F

"Reading Joshua Hull's grief-rot-opera *8 1 1 4* is akin to uncovering that lost VHS tape at the far back of the Blockbuster video, all scuzzed up with nowhere to go but straight into the cassette player of your brain. This is opaque horror, this is black mold horror, this is the hole at the center of Hull's own heart and it's swallowed me up."

— Clay McLeod Chapman, author of
Wake Up and Open Your Eyes

"*8 1 1 4* is a speeding car with no brakes on a road going straight into Hell. A brutal tale of how narcissism and ego in today's technology-driven world can conjure the very worst kinds of evil, then give it a microphone."

— Philip Fracassi, author of *Boys in*
the Valley

"Dripping with guilt and grief, heartbreak and hope, Joshua Hull has achieved something special here, a blend of the haunted self and the haunted house narrative. *8 1 1 4* leaves a mark, a scar that will leave readers lost in thought, reflecting on the authenticity of their own memories."

— Michael J. Seidlinger, author of
Anybody Home?* and *The Body
Harvest

8114

HORROR

8114
Copyright © 2025 by Joshua Hull
Cover by: Joel Amat Güell
Interior art by: Shannon Hull
ISBN: 9781960988607 (paperback)

CLASH Books
Troy, NY
clashbooks.com
Distributed by Consortium.
All rights reserved.

First Edition 2025
Printed in the United States of America.

For everyone who grew up a little haunted...
...and tried to leave their ghosts behind.

8114

Joshua Hull

HORROR

PART ONE
ADAM

Adam Benny is Missing – Episode 7
May 20th, 2025

Hey there listeners.

It's Paul Early... and this is Episode 7 of **Adam Benny is Missing**. I don't know if we can even call this an episode number. It's more of an update on the podcast about, well, I don't really know anymore. It's May 17*th* and this episode will air on May 20*th*... so whatever happens between this recording and the air date **will not** be addressed. And that... could be a lot of things.

By now, most of you have seen the post on social media. And know that Adam Benny did NOT go missing in junior high. He wasn't the victim of any sort of nefarious behavior... like kidnapping or murder.

He's alive and well.

Turns out, Adam and his mom, Sheila, left Indiana to allegedly get out of an extremely abusive and dangerous relationship with Adam's father. I say "allegedly" because we don't actually know if this was the case... AND because I **don't** want to get sued by Carl Benny.

Rumor has it, that by doing this podcast, I have put Adam and his mother's peaceful and quiet life in jeopardy. Which... was never my intent. My only goal with this show was to try *and find a missing classmate. And instead, I have... well, to put it plainly,* **fucked up**.

I **really** *fucked up.*

I want to sincerely apologize for any damage I have done and if I've misled any of you through the first six episodes of this podcast. Again, that was never, **ever** *my intent.*

I want to apologize to Producer Rachel who has been unfairly roped into my bullshit. And finally, I want to apologize to Adam and his family for disrupting their lives. I feel terrible, and I don't know what else to say.

I'm truly sorry.

I will be taking some time away from this podcast to take a deep look at myself and to try and make amends with Adam and his family. We have offered to give him the floor with an upcoming episode, but he is understandably **NOT** *interested in doing that. If that changes, we'll let you know. In the meantime, look for updates on this feed if you're interested or even still listening. I can't imagine there's many of you left.*

And I don't blame you.

Again, I apologize for any pain or damage I have caused with my reckless behavior. Stay safe and be well. Bye for now.

Paul Early, signing off.

Chapter One

I've always been a talker.

Some people say it's my superpower. Others say I should talk less. Like, *way* less. I admit, it was a problem growing up. My teachers weren't exactly fans of having me in class. There's nothing quite like trying to get through a discussion of Lewis and Clark with the constant murmuring of my prepubescent voice providing an annoying soundtrack.

It led to quite a few visits to the hallway. And to the principal's office. And to me trying to explain to my mother why I just couldn't seem to keep my mouth shut.

"I just like to talk. And others around me like to listen. So, it just makes sense to blabber."

And it did make sense once I got into high school and took Radio One. Our campus was known for having one of the best school radio stations in the state. *"We're the cream of the local crop!"* Mr. Barry would say, letting his red-tinted-nose glow with pride. The station would of course broadcast all the high school sports activities BUT they also had students as actual deejays. Nothing says *cool high schooler* quite like spinning Frankie Valli and the Four Seasons records.

But here's the thing... it *was* cool. And after I graduated, the station got even cooler. They switched formats and started playing the Billboard Top 100. Goodbye The Monkees, hello "Poker Face" fourteen times a day. Fifteen times if some down-in-the-dumps teen needed the extra Gaga pick-me-up.

Unfortunately, that high school radio station was the closest I ever got to being a "real" disc jockey. Unless you count my "elementary career day" thrift store costume of Casey Kasem. But I doubt that *you* or anyone else does. Nobody even knew who I was supposed to be dressed up as. It was a total bomb.

An American Flop 40.

And that's how my "radio career" stayed. I couldn't even get a job at a local radio station mailroom. Thank goodness for the invention of podcasts. And thank God or whoever you worship for amateur sleuths who would crack the true crime subgenre wide open with the format.

Everyone was doing it!

A ton of Sherlock home studios gave way to an entire boom of podcasts investigating unsolved murders and mysterious disappearances. Cold cases became hot, and everyone became a crime expert overnight. *Or...* at least they thought they did. There are know-it-alls and then there are know-nothing-at-alls.

Regrettably, you can plant *me* square in that second group.

Now that I think back on what happened and how everything played out, maybe I shouldn't have been so quick to dip my toes into that world. So quick to think that I could maybe make some sort of difference with my limited knowledge and technical experience.

Honestly, I have no idea what in the hell I was thinking.

I never had much interest in being any sort of "detective" type, outside of dressing up as Batman once or twice for Halloween. I also never had any desire to try to figure out any kind of lingering unsolved mystery. As a matter of fact, that show scared the shit out of me as a child. I still have nightmares about Robert Stack's cold camera stare and that haunting quote of his; *Join me. Perhaps next time,* **you** *may be able to help solve a mystery.*

Perhaps not.

Perhaps a podcast was a *very* bad idea. But on the other hand, it was a *much* simpler one. I had zero interest in holding down a day job like most of my friends. And I *really* liked the idea of money. So obviously, I was the next logical choice in the pyramid of people trying to find their footing in the true crime podcast realm.

And yes, clearly, it's a *very* bad idea to admit doing something solely because you thought it could make money. Especially with the way my get rich (*ermm, get broke, piss off a lot of people*) scheme ended. But here's the thing. It wasn't really a scheme at all. And it wasn't me just doing *something* for the hell of doing it.

I *really* was curious about what happened to Adam Benny.

He sat next to me in Mrs. Campbell's homeroom for the entire first half of seventh grade. It's easy to say that he was a shy, awkward kid, but honestly? It was seventh grade. We were all shy and awkward... but Adam?

He *was* different.

He didn't know about things like the rest of us. I'm not talking like, science or math. I mean more like... he didn't know about things happening in the world of kids our age. There was no TGIF for him. Forget Super Nintendo, Adam didn't even know about *regular* Nintendo.

The only music he listened to was Sandy Patty. And sure, I get it. She lived one town over from us and sang the word of the gospel. But this was 1994. There were only three TRUE gospels to sing along with that year: Weezer's *Blue Album*, Toadies' *Rubberneck*, and Nirvana's *MTV Unplugged in New York.*

During lunch period, I would let Adam listen to music on my Sony Discman. He didn't know any of the songs from

those albums. No *Possum Kingdom*. Forget Kurt and compa-
ny's cover of *The Man Who Sold the World*. No chance in hell
that he knew about Bowie's version. Not even *Undone – The
Sweater Song*, which is arguably still one of the greatest songs
ever made BUT was a song that saw **major** radio play. How
had he *not* heard it??

He listened to Rivers Cuomo sing about his sweater for
the first time over a plate of Salisbury steak and lunch lady
peas.

And it wasn't just that song or those three albums. He
didn't know any of the new music I played for him that year.
*Nine Inch Nails. Green Day. Notorious B.I.G. Hole. Beastie
Boys. The Offspring. Outkast.*

Every single lunch period was a new musical experience
for him. Don't even get me started on movies. He didn't know
one quote from *Ace Ventura: Pet Detective* or *The Mask*.
Come to think about it, I don't even know if Adam Benny
knew who the hell Jim Carrey was.

How was that even possible in 1994??

I was trying my best to give him a lesson in pop culture.
Or at least, what a twelve-year-old thought pop culture was.
He started smiling more and laughing his weird, awkward
laugh. You could tell he was still trying to figure out exactly
how to make a "laugh" work, which... yeah, I always thought it
was a little strange. But I just chalked it up to him being shy
and awkward.

A little different than the rest of us.

Turns out, it was something much worse. Around March
of the next year, Adam showed up to school covered in
bruises. These weren't the kind you got from roughhousing
with a sibling, or the kind that were easily covered with the
pull of a sweatshirt sleeve.

His face was completely swollen, like he was cosplaying
as *The Elephant Man*, and he sat at our two-person lunch
table with a noticeable hunch. Every move he made hurt as if
he was in pain just existing.

Clearly, he was.

He stared down at the cafeteria table and shuffled the spoon around inside of his yogurt container. Apparently, it was the only thing he could eat that "didn't hurt." I didn't know how to respond so I did the only thing I could think of. I pulled out my Discman and slid it across the table. He slowly looked up and kept his battered hands away from the device.

"Not today."

At the time, I was damn near thirteen years old so I wouldn't know an obvious sign if it smacked me in the face. Clearly, I wouldn't even know if said sign smacked *him* in the face. I was oblivious... and a terrible listener.

I pushed the CD player closer to him.

"This is a good one. It will help." I said, urging the hurting kid to give it a try. Adam looked up at me, tears in the corners of his blackened, downtrodden eyes.

"Wh... what is it?"

I popped open the lid of the device and showed him the disc patiently waiting for his ears. He looked down at the silver CD with a small purple circle at the top, and a lower-case "r" in the middle. I grinned—

"It's the new *Radiohead*. *The Bends*."

Adam nodded at me and slowly closed the lid of the walkman. He lightly placed the headphones over his head, careful not to touch any of the swelling. Then, I pressed play and we both watched as the CD spun to life.

Now, I'd like to think "*Planet Telex*" changed everything for Adam Benny that day. That Thom Yorke's lyrics about how *everything and everyone is broken* saved his life. But the truth is, they didn't.

They never even had a chance.

He didn't even get to the first bridge before Principal Ballard and Counselor Levy approached our table. Adam pulled off the headphones and set them on the table, "*Planet Telex*" still playing. Then, he nodded at me, slowly pulled himself out of his chair and walked away with the two adults.

I put the headphones on and let Thom's voice provide the soundtrack for the moment.

Everything *was* broken.

That was the last time I ever saw Adam Benny. A bruised and beaten thirteen-year-old being escorted out of the cafeteria while hundreds of other students watched. And none of us said anything about it. Until I launched that goddamn podcast.

Sigh.

I knew something was wrong after the fourth email. It didn't have the same friendly, "asking" tone of the three that came before it. It was just one threatening sentence—

*"I have asked and asked... but you continue to ignore me. If you do not stop this podcast, there **will be** consequences, Paul."*

Producer Rachel laughed it off, much like she had with the other ones. She had experience in True Crime podcasts before we launched *Adam Benny is Missing*. Before we had around three thousand or so strangers listening to us every episode. It wasn't like she was winning Webby Awards or anything, but she had way more experience in the field than I did. And way more experience dealing with anonymous threats.

"I remember we kept getting emails from someone named Jeb when we were doing *Heartland Harvest*. That was the one about a missing lady they found naked and dead in some random cornfield." Rachel was so casual about the subject matter of these things. Come to think about it, she was so casual about *everything*. Especially *Heartland Harvest*, the podcast she did before ours.

She had a habit of explaining the events to myself and others like she was summing up a long-lost episode of *Friends* or something—

"So... in walks Joey and right there, in the middle of Central Perk is just this dead, naked woman. He takes a sip of his coffee and asks the body, "How you doin'?" The audience is laughing.

*I'm laughing. It seems like the only person **not** laughing is the dead lady."*

Something tells me it's because of the subject matter.

You have to look at it through rose-colored glasses, so it doesn't beat you down... or make you lose faith in humanity. That's what I like to think anyway. She *might* just be damaged as hell with a sick and twisted sense of humor.

Whatever it was, I always found it oddly comforting when reading anonymous reviews online or reading threatening, anonymous emails.

"Jeb would email us after every new episode. Telling us we were wrong about certain facts with the case. We messed up the description of the body. Or... our crime scene layout was all screwed up. We start to assume that Jeb *is* the killer, mad that we're fucking with his legacy. Turns out... Jeb was just some little shit-bag kid who saw two horny adults go into the cornfield together. So, he followed them and hid just out of sight, watching everything as the stalks swayed all around him. He saw *everything!* And... our friend Jeb was working on his own podcast about the case. *He Who Talks Behind the Rows* or some bullshit title like that. Clearly, he wasn't talking behind anything if he waited all this time, you know? Point is, you've got your own Jeb, Pauly. Laugh it off."

I couldn't just laugh it off though.

I never stopped thinking about *Jeb* after hearing that story. Not because of what he did, but because of what he was *planning* on doing. He was the sole eyewitness to an unsolved crime, and he was going to take that knowledge and do a podcast with information he *most definitely* withheld from the police.

He was planning on spilling secrets to listeners world-wide. No matter the consequences. No matter who got hurt. He was going to do it for his own personal gain. Rachel was right, there was a Jeb, but I didn't have one.

I was one.

A few hours after a rather explosive, albeit revealing,

episode six of *Adam Benny is Missing* went up, a brand new, egged profile picture Twitter account tweeted out a damning twenty-three-word tweet:

Adam Benny is NOT missing

He WAS surviving.

Paul Early is LYING. And he has put my family in extreme danger.

More soon...

Rachel tried to laugh off the tweet as *"Just another Jeb situation"* ... but I knew better. Not because of how viral the tweet went afterwards or because of the *angry* reaction online. Or all the comments that flooded our podcast feed. I knew it wasn't a Jeb situation because I knew it was *him*.

I knew it was Adam Benny. And he *wanted* me to know it **was** him with the account username.

@adambends

There were only two people in the world that knew we listened to Radiohead's *The Bends* the last time we saw each other. And one of them was no longer missing. One of them never *went* missing. They were just trying to survive, and the other one fucked it all up with a dumb podcast. Producer Rachel couldn't laugh that one off.

And she still hasn't.

Social media struck back with a fury we had only seen directed at shamed politicians and sex creep Hollywood moguls. There was only one way to get out of it. I recorded the final "episode" of *Adam Benny is Missing* on May 17th. It went live on May 20th.

One day later, I received a frantic phone call asking me to come home as soon as possible...

E very town has that one bar that you hear about from
        third grade on.
                Pendleton was no different. Ours was a little
hole in the wall in the middle of town called Donnie's Place.
A small, musky joint that seemed like it could hold every resident on Friday or Saturday nights. You could walk by on the
weekends and hear the laughing, yelling, and occasional
violence spilling out through the open door.

I remember strolling by with some friends on one particularly rowdy Friday night to see our middle school English
teacher dancing at the bar. At least, it seemed like dancing.
Her body was loose and gyrating, and there was music. So...
dancing! Upon closer inspection, it seemed like she was
getting frisky with a pair of men that heavily resembled the
Beyond Thunderdome duo of "Master-Blaster." We couldn't
confirm the authenticity of that due to Mrs. Jackson from
Social Studies shooing us away in a hurry.

"This place is not for you!"

Her words ricocheted around in my head. *"This place is
not for you!"* ... like Mrs. Jackson was a member of some sort of
secret organization dedicated to "The Secret of Donnie."
How dare a mere mortal like me try to catch a glimpse of the

belligerent, animalistic activities of these adult townies. If that's how our *teachers* acted there, we all wondered how our parents acted. How *we* would act once we were able to cross over the invisible barrier that always kept us out of Alcohol Narnia.

Long story short, pretty much the same exact way.

I celebrated my twenty-first birthday at Donnie's. And while I didn't spend it writhing about with Master-Blaster, my mother thought it would be funny for my first *legal* drink of alcohol to be a shot called a "blowjob." Even better, she thought an eighty-year-old woman should give me that shot of Kahlua, Baileys, and Amaretto.

Yes, I celebrated one of my most important birthdays with my mom. And yes, one of her favorite stories to tell is how she got me a blowjob from an eighty-year-old woman. It's one of the only things I still remember from that night.

It quickly turned into a blur, that then turned into a vomit-inducing hangover the next day. I was now an official member of "The Secret of Donnie." And I would attend regular "meetings" there with my best friends Matt, Kyle, and Glenn. We were sort of like the drunken version of *The Goonies*. I say sort of because instead of looking for one, we did our absolute best to avoid *any* One-Eyed-Willy we would possibly find at Donnie's.

Each night, we had a new hazy, blurry, drunken adventure. There were fights, run-ins with old classmates or exes, drunken karaoke sessions with former teachers, and we sampled every style of alcohol behind the bar.

Even the Malört.

That one made us all gag then... and makes me want to gag now just thinking about it. Occasionally, we would peer out the open front door of Donnie's Place. And through the rims of our light beers or shots of Jägermeister, we'd find a curious group of pre-teens gazing at us from the seats of their bikes.

Like a time-capsule stuck in drying cement, we were those

kids once. Bikes parked and curiosity perked. There seemed to be a bit of old magic to this place and a whole lot of questions. Twenty-something years later, we knew all the answers to what was waiting just beyond Donnie's doorway.

Old, stained tile. Broken lock bathrooms with doorless stalls. The smell of built-up grease and alcohol. Terrible live music from *Fleetwood Mac* wannabes. Cheap merchandise that only the booziest of locals would buy. The Polaroid pictures on the wall of patrons and staff. The memories and the overwhelming sense of regret and missed opportunities.

That was Donnie's Place.

We now knew everything, or at least we thought we did.

That was until the moment I found myself once again standing in the open doorway of Donnie's. And once again, I was a curious kid wondering just what the hell was waiting for me on the other side. The answer was mostly judgmental eyes and the sort of faces that screamed a variety of unsaid thoughts like—

"What's he doing here?"

"He's back home?"

"Who the hell is this person?"

It was sort of like I was a contestant on a new game show called **"How Uncomfortable Would You Feel Walking into Your Hometown Bar for The First Time in Ten Years?"** The title obviously needs work... but it's one helluva concept for an entertaining TV show.

If it starred *someone else.*

I made my way to the back of the bar, the place we always chose to be. Away from the live music, away from the front door, and right next to the shitty, unlocked bathrooms. It was the perfect spot to talk and drink the night away. Judging by the lowered buzzed head of a man holding onto a full pint, it still was.

"That doesn't look like vodka and Dew."

Matt looked up at me and forced a smile from ear to ear. It was like nothing had changed on him. The same youthful face and the same shit-eating grin that filled every scruffy inch of his face.

"Sure as hell doesn't taste as good as one either," he said.

I laughed, *gagged*, off the comment as he stood up from the booth to give me a hug. We embraced like two old war buddies, if war consisted of nonstop partying and hangovers. He pulled away and went right back to his seat to caress his beer. The head had gone down considerably... which told me he had been holding onto that glass for some time. Judging by the deep look in his eyes, it wasn't the beer he was so desperate to hold onto.

We hadn't seen each other in almost three years.

Or was it longer than that?

We still talked and texted on a regular basis but there's at least four hundred miles between our houses. He was a family man now and I was just a fuckup back home for—

It suddenly dawned on me that I had no idea why I was back home. Why I was currently standing in the back of Donnie's Place again, waiting for an old classmate to take my order. Most importantly, I had no idea why Matt had a lost, terrified look in his eyes. I assumed we would get to that eventually. For now, it was back to the basics—

"How's the family?"

He gave a few eager nods.

"Good. They're all good. Football. Gymnastics. They keep me busy. You know how it goes."

He glanced up at me, then shook his head like it was completely empty. *Shit.*

"You *don't* know how it goes. Sorry, man. My head is all screwy." He remarked. I slid into the booth and nodded.

"All good," I said, trying my best to make sure he knew he hadn't offended me by forgetting I don't have kids. Or a wife. Or... anyone really. I have me, myself, and I... and we're doing just fine.

Right.

Maybe fine isn't the word.

We're just barely scraping by.

The bartender popped over and glanced at both of us through a cloud of irritation. That feeling clearly wasn't directed at Matt since he had been here drinking already. I could tell by her eyes and her face... and well, the language of her *entire* body that it was all because of *me* being in this booth.

"What are you having?" She said with displeasure seeping out every pore. I looked at her, side ponytail hanging off her head. The only thing missing was a big hunk of chewing gum that she could chomp loudly in my face.

And maybe a pink leather jacket and a musical number.

I looked at Matt's nearly full pint and pointed down at it.

"That looks great," I said. "I'll take one."

A long sigh fell out of her mouth and her head fell over to Matt's side of the table.

"Do you remember what you ordered?"

He grinned. "Beer."

She shook her head and stomped off to the safety of her bar. We both watched as she tapped a few buttons on the POS screen then aggressively grabbed an empty pint glass. She swung back around and placed the rim of the glass under the tap and poured a golden ale into it. Intentional foam filled the glass and overflowed out into the drain. We held our laughter in as long as we could.

Until the goddamn Humor Dam busted.

"She doesn't like you," Matt said, in his best Dr. Evazan voice. It made me wonder if our bartender had a friend, and if they both had the death sentence on twelve systems. I gave her another look, foam still overflowing from the glass.

"Who is that again?" I asked.

"Sheila Thomas."

I glanced at Sheila Thomas pouring my beer, anticipating a spit bomb.

Any minute now.

"No. Fucking. Way. That can't be **her**."

Matt took a large sip of his beer, then wiped a bit from his beard as he set the glass down.

"*Sheila Feeela*," he sang, clearly loud enough for the poor bartender to hear. I hid my laughter by covering the side of my face with my hand. *Holy shit.* Sheila Feeela, in the flesh.

"Didn't Jake...?" I asked.

"Yep. In the back of his truck. Right after Andy Jones," he said with a huge grin.

"Jesus."

"No, not *him.* She kept screaming about his dad though."

The joke sailed over my head until the moment Sheila dropped off my beer. My laughter spilled out all over the tabletop, which *probably* didn't help her swirling cloud of irritation. I slid the fresh pint over in front of me and raised it to my lips.

"Thank you."

Instead of walking away, Sheila Thomas just stared down at me and my elevated beer.

"You know, you were always an asshole. But what you did to Aaron Benny is like... next level asshole."

Matt watched as she walked away, then looked over at me... almost as if he was expecting me to retaliate in some form. But I just slowly sipped on my beer and grinned.

"What?" he asked.

"I might be an asshole. But at least I know his name was **Adam Benny**," I said.

Matt let out a loud laugh and shook his head in Sheila's direction.

"That's fucked up," he snickered.

We both took a sip of our beer and sat in silence.

"That whole situation is fucked up, man." He said, giving me a look of friendly disappointment. "You want to talk about it?"

Not really. Truth be told, I was tired of talking about it. I dedicated an entire podcast to talking about the Adam Benny situation. In my eyes, there was nothing for me to talk about anymore. It was time for everyone to move on from it.

"Nope. I'm just sort of... over it. Ready for it all to be in the past."

Matt took another sip from his beer and raised his eyebrow.

"Good luck with that. People are pretty pissed-off about it 'round here."

"They'll be fine," I said, raising my own glass. "Plus, this town gets mad about everything. There will be something else next week for the gossip hounds to focus on."

"Yeah, about that." He sighed and leaned back into the booth. I took another look into his eyes. That haunted gaze was back and so was my curiosity. I set my glass down on the table and took a long, deep breath.

"So... come on. Why'd you beg me to come back home?"

He looked up at me, confusion flooding his entire face.

"Wait, you don't know?" He asked.

"The only thing I know... is you called and asked me to come home as soon as possible. I immediately hopped in my car and drove eight hours straight to meet you here for a beer." I threw my hands up. "So, Matt. *Why* am I here?"

His hands clamped around the edges of his pint glass and his knuckles turned red. I kept waiting for the glass to explode under the pressure, but it never did. Instead, his eyes burst under it. Tears streamed down his cheeks, and he looked up at me, red-faced and scared. Like he didn't want to tell me something, but he couldn't hold it in any longer—

"Kyle is gone, man."

I stared at his watering eyes, unsure of what type of gone Matt was referring to here.

"What do you mean?"

"He killed himself, Paul."

The statement hit me in the face like a bag of bricks. Of all the things I was expecting to come out of Matt's mouth, the death of our best friend was not one of them. *And suicide?* How the hell was that even possible?

Kyle was happy. He had a family, and they were building a life together. *Had* a life together! I found myself gripping my pint glass with the same amount of strength and pain that Matt was.

"What do you mean? *When?*"

"Two days ago," he said.

"How?"

Matt wiped another round of tears from his face and leaned in closer.

"He shot himself."

"No. That can't be real," I said, shaking my head at the thought. He nodded, agreeing wholeheartedly with me.

Did Kyle even own a gun? Hell, did he even know how to use one? Or did that even matter if he was just looking to use it one time. It was all too much for me to think about. To even process. To even—

"It doesn't... *this* doesn't make sense, man," I said.

"I know. That's why I asked you to come home," he whimpered.

"For what? To help with the funeral?"

He vigorously shook his head. *Not really.*

"Sure, yeah. That would help but no, that's not the main reason," he said.

"Then why?"

Matt looked at me with his scared, bloodshot eyes—

"Because he did it at your old house."

Chapter Three

The alcohol was strong on my breath the next morning.

I was in my clothes from the night before... and my head still felt every drink. My heart still felt every word. Kyle was *really* gone... and I spent my entire night drinking that fact away. Trying to convince my brain that it was all a dream. Trying to get lost in the memories. Hell, maybe just lost in general.

I looked around the room to make sure I was where I was supposed to be. Cheesy "home" décor hung from the walls and cheap coffee packets sat waiting. A "thank you" gift from the host. A small, generic Airbnb; I was where I was supposed to be.

Whatever the hell that meant.

Pendleton wasn't exactly a tourist destination even though we're a designated "historical" site in the state. Still, it blew my mind that it now had several listings on all the short-term homestay websites. We're at least forty-five minutes from the city, which means if you bring your family, that's at least forty-five minutes away from the closest zoo, state museums, professional sports arenas, and the world-famous racetrack.

Sure, you could travel up north about ten minutes up the highway and find a casino and a small racetrack made famous by HBO years ago. But those don't exactly scream "family friendly." Our town at least had a park you could walk to in less than five minutes and fill an entire day with the playgrounds, waterfall, trails, and public swimming pool. Then there were all the local shops and restaurants lining the main strip of town.

There was ice cream, a shop dedicated to apple butter and other farm friendly wares, the previously mentioned Donnie's Place, a traditional family restaurant, a flower boutique, a toy store where the owners dress like Christmas elves, multiple antique shops, a donut chain, and more salons than you can count on one hand. We used to have more variety like an old movie theater, a baseball card shop, and even a used bookstore once upon a time. We also now had a locally owned coffee roastery that was right across the street from my temporary apartment... and it was loudly calling my name.

I spent the rest of the morning driving around my old stomping grounds. Not out of curiosity for what else had changed over the last ten years, but to process the news about Kyle. There was a calming nature to seeing some of our old haunts and thinking about our youthful shenanigans. But that peace was soon interrupted by the realization that he was *actually* gone. *Forever*. It was hard to wrap my head around that for multiple reasons.

Like I said, Kyle was a family man. He and his wife Amber just welcomed a new baby into the world not even a year ago. I remember quickly scrolling past the latest round of family portraits they had done six months ago.

Kyle in a traditional "dad" polo and khaki shorts. His trademark goofy smile as his hand wrapped around the waist of Amber. Their seven-year-old Autumn—*or was she eight or nine now*—sat smiling in front of them. Amber held the newborn baby—*Kelly? Emily?*—in her arms. She was crying, much like babies do. But they all seemed happy.

He seemed happy.

Or maybe he didn't. It suddenly dawned on me that Kyle called me two days ago. The same day he decided to—*damn.*

I didn't answer... and I never listened to the voicemail he left. I now wonder if I even should. Was it his farewell? Was he just calling to joke around about something? Or was it something else entirely? My body trembled at the thought of pushing play on the message, not because of what might be waiting for me on the other end. But because of what I already knew was there—

The last message I would *ever* get from Kyle Robinson.

That was hard to process, so I pulled into the empty parking lot of what used to be our small-town grocery store, *Bill's Market.* I looked at the old building that housed a ton of childhood memories. Food shopping with my mom, the smell of fresh, baked donuts, and running up and down each aisle with my friends during summer break, causing ruckus for anyone in our way. Usually getting yelled at to "Get on out of here!" by Mike, the shopping cart wrangler. And we *would* "get on out" after tossing our "football" loaves of bread back on the shelf and wagging our tongues at the poor man.

Bill's Market was replaced by a much larger regional chain who built a brand-new location out by the high school. Right across from the new, to me, Taco Bell and Wendy's. The new grocery spot was *way* more convenient for stay-at-home moms who could drop their kids off at school, then pop over across the street for their morning errands. Less convenient for wild, trouble-making kids who wanted to play toss with a couple loaves of bread.

Also, super convenient for parking lot ponder sessions.

Bill's old grocery skeleton stared back at me. It was now used as a consignment store or something. I couldn't really tell from where I parked at the back of the lot. I looked out my window into the small-town that shaped my life. Liquor store behind me. A new bagel spot where the old Chinese restaurant was. A bank across the street. Town Hall on the corner.

A different memory played out in my head regardless of the direction I looked.

This place has changed so much.

I... *have* changed so much.

As I held up my phone, I couldn't help but get the feeling that everything was about to change again. And not for the better. I looked down at the screen, catching a glimpse of missed calls, unread texts, and emails. The red notification of a waiting voicemail stared back... so I clicked the icon.

I should have **never** listened to it.

The first thing to greet my ears was Kyle's familiar voice, normal and happy.

Hey Bud,

Just calling to... check in. We haven't talked in a bit, so I wanted to see how you're doing with everything. I also wanted to let you know—

Suddenly, a low hum of garbled feedback took over. It slowly grew louder and louder, until it screamed out like pissed-off white noise. I had to pull the phone away for a moment, startled by the unsettling sounds. Once they died off, I brought the phone back to the side of my head.

That's when he started talking again.

*I know none of this makes sense to you. But it will soon. It will **all** make sense soon. The sins of the past... they spread like mold. Contaminating the present. Poisoning the future... like an infected well. This place is hungry... and it wants **you** back, Paul. It's waiting for the last one... and so am I.*

The angry white noise returned for a moment—

Bye for now. And just remember, friend... don't forget to clear your head. To give your life and join the dead. To close your eyes and join the black.

His voice took on a demented tone—

*The things out **there**, they want you back.*

I dropped the phone from my hand just as the horrific whispers and laughter started echoing Kyle's message. Now... I can't be positive because the voice of my dead best friend just spooked the absolute hell out of me, so I was a bit on edge. But I'm almost sure that the glowing screen of my cell phone became a disgusting strain of spreading black mold.

The terrifying whispers suddenly took over the entire interior of my car. It was all too much, so I stumbled out of my driver's side door and fell onto the black pavement ass first. The car radio suddenly kicked on and Kyle and the gaggle of horrific back up voices echoed his voicemail—

Bye for now. And just remember, friend... don't forget to clear your head. To give your life and join the dead. To close your eyes and join the black. The things out there, they want you back.

The morning sun revealed an approaching shadow... so I spun around, hoping a random townie didn't catch the current shitshow. Much to my surprise, the oncoming shadow *was* the current shitshow.

I stared up at newly dead Kyle Robinson.

The stringy side of his head hung loose, revealing brain matter and gore. I kept expecting the chunk of dead face to fall off and tumble down the side of his cheek, but it never did. He—*it?*—just stared down at me, dumbstruck with awe at the sight of me on the pavement.

"What the—" I screamed out.

Kyle's mouth fell open, like the detached chin of a ventriloquist dummy. Much like his face and head, his voice was no longer that of my best friend. It was now of something else entirely. Deep and mutated, accompanied by a tacked-on hiss—

"*It wants you back, Paul.*"

"Who?" I asked, disoriented as hell. Quickly finding myself settling down into piss-your-pants territory. The fresh dead face of my friend grinned; blood lined his damaged teeth.

"*It's time for you to come back home.*"

"I am home! Because of you!"

Dead Kyle licked away a chunk of gore and smiled.

"*Not because of me. Because of* **you**. *Because of them.* **All of them**..."

His final word hissed on forever. It was an unbearable sound that terrified every ounce of my body. I was frozen in fear until... the loud bang of a car door slamming shut pulled my attention away. I turned to see an elderly woman staring down at me in confusion.

"You okay, young man?"

I looked at her, then back at my empty car. It was silent as can be. No whispers, no eerie white noise. I looked around, no dead Kyle. Just me sitting in the parking lot of an old grocery store looking like a damn fool.

"There... was a spider," I exclaimed.

I watched her eye the interior of my car... then my chaotic, terrified face. I moved to cover my crotch in case it *was* wet.

"Must've been a big one."

I nodded. *You have no idea.*

She locked her car and made her way to the front doors of the consignment shop. After a moment of collecting myself, I stood up and peered into the open door of the car. Even though Kyle had been outside with me, I absolutely checked the backseat. *Luckily, no dead ghoul friend.*

I crawled back into the driver's seat and took a long, deep breath.

It suddenly hit me.

I knew what Kyle meant when he told me it's time to come back home. He didn't mean this town. He meant the place I grew up: **8114 South State Road 67**. And judging by what I just experienced in the old Bill's parking lot—

I had no idea what would be waiting for me.

Death was a permanent resident at 8114 long before Kyle decided he would redecorate it with the interior of his head.

Ruin. Decay. Rot.

It was all practically built into the foundation of that old house. And all eight acres of the withered, surrounding land. Whatever came across it would experience either a quick, painful death... or a slow spreading demise.

Like a homegrown cancer.

Didn't matter if it was alive... or inanimate. If it arrived at 8114, it was doomed. Family pets. Stray animals. Birds, rabbits, possums. We had so many random, grotesque animal deaths that we had to build a "pet cemetery" behind one of the barns.

It's like that book said, sometimes dead *is* better.

But also... sometimes the dead pile up so much, that you have to expand the land you buried your favorite dog in just to be able to fit the carcass of a skinny, malnourished raccoon. So, I don't know if death *is* better if my old Saint Bernard has to spend the afterlife laying next to a creature that could kill you with one infected bite.

But again... this was 8114.

Everything seemed to be infected.

Car batteries. Brand new electronics. It was like the house was powered by the energizer death bunny. Relationships. Friendships. Random strangers. It didn't matter who, or what, it was.

One time, an older man pulled into our long, oval-shaped driveway to ask my stepfather Hank a question. I stumbled over, as curious kids often do, and the man delivered a kind wave in my direction with his long, thin right hand. He had a slight, nervous tic in his index finger.

"A bit lost. My eyesight ain't what it used to be!"

The man wasn't there longer than five minutes, gathering directions to a local church he couldn't find, or one he already found but couldn't see. Hank soon waved him on his way. The man pulled out onto the highway and up over the hill the railroad tracks sat on. His car died just as the loud, approaching horn of a speeding train screamed out.

I knew Hank could run fast, but *that* was the fastest I've ever seen *anyone* run. And in the end, it didn't matter. Not even Barry Allan could have saved the old man from *that* impact. Crushed metal, shattered lives. One of Hank's favorite Hawaiian shirts covered in a stranger's blood.

I spent the rest of the day inside and that night staring out over the cleaned-up tracks from my bedroom window. I swear I saw what was left of the old man waving at me from the tracks. His body was entirely caved in on the left side... and his remaining right half waved his long, thin hand at me.

Nervous index finger tic and all...

After that day, I knew something was seriously off with our old farmhouse at 8114. And after what Kyle did, I now know it never truly stops spreading its disease to whoever was there. The cancer never truly goes into remission, it just lays dormant until it's ready to show itself again.

I wonder what the spread looks like inside of me.

Are my lungs filled with black mold? Is my throat filled with infected screams that I never let out? What about my brain... or my eyes? Everything I'd seen or thought, poisoned by a house with no remorse. It just wants to eat. It only has a hunger for death.

I couldn't shake the thought.

What did the inside of my body look like after spending eighteen years there? And most importantly, when would the infection rear its ugly head again? When would 8114 growl and gnash its demented, abandoned teeth at me?

It's hungry, Paul.

That bit of Kyle's voicemail stuck out to me. 8114 was ready to feed again. Like it always had. Or... had it?

Maybe all of this was just a big coincidence tied to misremembered experiences of our youth. Kids say the darndest things... and sometimes they *think they see* the darndest things. Maybe Kyle's death is just a terrible tragedy that has latched on to my guilt about Adam Benny. Maybe I want all of this to be so much more than what it truly is:

A piece of shit dealing with all the shit he left behind.

I pulled my car into what used to be the entrance of 8114 and turned it off. I gazed out the passenger side window at the makeshift forest now covering the remnants of the house. A chill traveled down my spine, and I thought about turning the key, and hightailing it out of there. Out of this entire town.

I was still thinking about Kyle's voicemail and the things he said about this place. And now, here I was... on the outskirts of hell, holding an "admit one" ticket.

Sigh.

I pulled the keys out of the ignition and stepped out of the vehicle. As semis and other traffic whizzed by behind me on the interstate, I leaned over the hood of the car and just stared into the abandoned grounds of my childhood. I wanted to close my eyes and see if it would be one of those moments where you hear the laughter of children and old memories coming to life. But I was too afraid of what I might see or hear when I closed them... so I just kept them open and focused on the dilapidated house.

This place was an active household for over twenty years. And that was just when *we* were here. That doesn't include the people who lived there before us. 8114 was home to multiple lives and legacies... and now, it was just an infected, swollen wound at the edge of town.

A wound you could barely get back to.

The town had placed a big mound of dirt in front of the oval driveway to keep vehicles and curious amateur investigators out. I couldn't help thinking about what they were trying to keep in. But... I know better than to think a small pile of IMI dirt is going to hold back whatever the hell *that* might be.

Mother Nature had reclaimed the house as much as she could. I pushed through the waist-high grass and swatted multiple bugs away from every inch of my body. I turned to take one last look at the safety of my car.

It's not too late.

It felt like a distant voice whispered out from the overgrown trees—***It is too late.***

Real or not, it was right.

I continued on my way through the front patch of the house. I used to take these same sweaty steps behind a push mower. This place could really use one of those right about now. *Hell, this place could use a miracle.*

I shoved my way through the draping trees doing their best to block the remainder of the driveway. One of the branches bent down and snagged me on my forearm, digging into my flesh with its aged bark. I took a few steps forward, all while surveying the damage on my skin. The wind picked up and pushed through the homegrown nature barrier. It seemed like the distant mysterious voice rang out again. This time doing its best Heather O'Rourke impression.

"*You're here...*"

I stopped dead in my tracks and looked up at the farmhouse, now staring back down at me. There was a brief moment where it felt like someone—*or something*—moved out of the empty doorway. I took another look down at my wounded arm—*was it bleeding more?*

"Shit."

I ripped a leaf from a nearby branch and wiped the fresh mess off my arm. I winced at the rough edge of the plant appendage. It tore as it went across the surface, a slither of green somehow disappearing into the fresh red wound.

"**SHIT.**"

The snap of a twig out by one of the barns pulled my attention back to the house. Somehow, it now looked as if 8114 had even more shrubs and trees engulfing it. Vines climbed along the exterior walls and spread onto the open spaces where our windows once lived.

I took a moment to think about all the times those windows were opened, either to let cigarette smoke escape or, *apologies for the unsanitary image*, to piss out of in the middle of the night. I can still remember Mom screaming about that one...

Now, those same windows just sat as if they were shocked by what has happened to them, with their open eyes and gaping mouths. Almost as if the house was wearing a rotted, screaming mask. You can practically hear the decrepit structure asking me... *why?*

Why was I left to fend for myself?

Why did you leave me alone to face a growing horror?

Some nearby laughter pulled my attention to the right, in the direction of the "new" Mexican restaurant that was literally a skip and a hop away from our old front yard. Nothing says "Patio margaritas!" quite like an abandoned farmhouse crumbling by the day.

If the Hacienda Hell House owners were true entrepreneurs, they would offer their customers a unique experience. A walking taco ghost tour where guests can munch on bags of Fritos and ground beef, all while the demons of 8114 catch a whiff of their on-the-go meal.

Sorry, no refunds for lifelong hauntings...

I focused back on the house and stepped onto the concrete front porch. I looked up at the empty frame of my old bedroom window and pictured another memory. Teenage versions of Kyle and Matt dropping water balloons on my head and falling back into the house laughing their asses off. I loved those guys.

I still do.

I peered into the open doorway, darkness hiding behind every inch of the frame.

And who the hell knows what else.

Old magazines and random papers littered the floor. The wallpapered walls were tattered and defaced. I could make out just a slight bit of graffiti on the wall of our old living room. That was the place we would have movie night or game night. And now it was just a free art space for random kids to tag things like **Mikey loves Jenny 4ever** or... **Billy likes butt stuff**.

There was more ruckus from the Mexican patio... and the sounds of someone screaming out *"Whoa, whoa, whoa!"* through their laughter.

Whoa, whoa, whoa.

Yep, that was a *very* clear sign for me to stay out of the house for now. I stepped off the porch and walked around the house, peering into the opened window of the front room as I moved. It was eerie... and sad. And every memory was suddenly shattered like the window.

I turned the corner and stared out at what remained of our four old barns.

There was the Old Garage at the far left. We used it for storage and parking older vehicles. It was mostly gone now.

Next to the garage was the Pig Barn. I fucking *hated* the pig barn. The first level of that creepy bastard is two-sided. One complete with pig stalls, and the other just a bare concrete room that led to a small loft. You could see into both sides through the cracks... and, well, *things* could see you. Just thinking about that creeped me the hell out.

Next to that was the Big Barn... and it earned that name by being just that, a big ass barn. It was two levels with multiple staircases and rooms for tractor storage and more. Looking at it now, I feel like we didn't do it enough justice by just calling it "big."

Gigantic. Colossal. Hell, Mega Barn would have been a perfect name.

That massive barn was where we spent most of our free time... **during the day**. You would never catch us in there after dark. Every summer we attempted to spend the night inside of it... and every summer we would chicken out and move all our sleeping bags back inside the house. Much to the complaints of everyone who wanted to have a peaceful night indoors.

Frankly put, Mega Barn was *Mega Scary as hell.*

Right outside of the base of the big barn, we had our makeshift basketball court. Then, next to that was the rarely entered Sheep Barn. Hank bought a boat once and just kept it in there. I laughed to myself, wondering if he ever took it out of there. Who buys a boat just to keep it docked inside of a barn? That's like Quint going to the town hall meeting in *Jaws* and scratching on the chalkboard, pulling everyone's attention:

"Boat goes in the water. You go in the water. Not my boat. Boats in the barn. Our barn."

Hank was an odd bird... but not as odd as that sheep barn. There was something... *off* about it. Like *something* wasn't happy that you were in there. It's a strange thing to feel unwelcome on your own property but that's exactly what it felt like inside that place.

And it was starting to feel like that again.

I decided I would start my flashback tour inside the Big Barn. Mostly, because I was curious about what was left behind in there. I assumed plenty of old toys, cassette tapes, and books would be waiting. There'd also be plenty of cracks, holes, and missing chunks inside the structure. This meant that it would stay lit up a decent amount of time... and light was a *good* thing out here.

I know, I know.

"A 42-year-old man basically just said he's scared of the dark."

But that's not true. I'm not scared of the dark at home, or anywhere else for that matter. I'm scared of the dark at 8114. I'm scared of a lot of things out at this place... which might explain why I jumped out of my skin when the barn door at the top of the hill suddenly slid open. Its rusty hinges crying out in ear-shattering pain.

I was *not* prepared for who walked out of it.

Chapter Five

"Paul Early."

I stared back at the oversized man looking back at me from the hill of the Big Barn. Less hair than I remember... but just about the same amount of body mass.

"...Officer Chip Allan."

He was the last person I expected to see here and the last person I expected to see *still* in *that* uniform. Last I heard, he was placed on leave for some anti-Muslim and anti-LGBTQIA+ rhetoric on Facebook.

"It's **Chief Chip Allan** now," he said back, with a shit-filled grin.

Chief?! *Goddamn.* This *is* small-town America.

"They made you Chief, huh?" I asked, with a very clear *what the fuck* inflection hanging on my voice.

"They *voted* me Chief," he proudly exclaimed.

I gave him a classic head nod and grinned—

"Even after the whole... what were they called again? *Memes?*"

He took a few steps down the hill, favoring one side of his aging body. Clearly, he was over people asking about the social media incident. And clearly, I didn't give a shit.

"Inappropriate jokes... which I apologized for. Turns out, public opinion speaks louder in voting booths than it does on the *out-to-get-ya* social media." I slightly flinched at the mention of the "out-to-get-ya" social media, mostly because it's still out there, *getting me*.

"I'd say so." I said, fake smiling as best as I could.

He blocked out the sun with his right hand, then extended his left one out to me.

"You *could* just say congrats. I'm sure I had your support out in... *wherever* you are," he said. Another nod, then I shook his hand.

"Congrats, Chief."

Our hands fell back to their rightful owners, and we stood in a moment of awkward silence. I looked up at the big barn door he just closed.

"So, what's a Chief like you doing in a place like this?"

He let out a small laugh.

"I think the better question is what are YOU doing here, Paul?"

Asking myself the same thing, Chief.

"I'm back home to see some friends. Is that against the law?"

Chief Allan took a *long* look around the broken-down property, then wiped the back of his balding head with his hand. A deep sigh escaped from his mouth.

"This place is off limits to the public," he declared.

"It's a good thing I'm not the public then, right?" The Chief looked me up and down.

Part of me could tell he wanted to load my ass up into his police cruiser and take me into town for everyone to see. The other part could tell that the man who had dedicated his entire life to serving and protecting this place was scared out of his mind. It felt like the fear was contagious around town all of a sudden. First Matt at the bar, and now Chief Allan out here.

Was there something in the water?

"It's just unsafe... and the town can't be held responsible for people getting hurt out here," he said, in a pleading voice.

"Last I checked, Hank and his dad still own the property. Seems like they'd be the ones to blame for people getting hurt," I said back. "I'd be fine with you holding them responsible for *anything* like that."

"Anything? What about people dying?" He hung his head, afraid to look me in my eyes. *Right.* **Kyle**. The weight and horror of why I showed up here came screaming back. It was all because of Kyle, same for the Chief. I looked around at the splintering, bare-boned existence of my early life.

"Where'd he do it at?"

The Chief looked up at me, not expecting the question. Not expecting any of *this*. You could see it in the way he walked around this place. And the way he looked at me. But expectations were a thing of the past, just like the grounds we stood on.

"Hell, Paul. You *really* want to know that?"

That was a loaded question. The very quick and obvious answer is *no.* **Hell no**. But the longer, more tangled answer is **YES**. I don't want to know as much as I *need* to know. More so, I need to understand why Kyle did what he did... *where* he did it. And what it has to do with me and this place.

What it has to do with *everything*.

Getting that answer would help. Not only me, but also maybe Chief Allan. Maybe it would help us both understand what happened here. I fought the urge to tell him about my run-in with Kyle's dead, talking body in town. About his last voicemail and the spreading mold. About all the questions I had... and all the answers I needed. But instead, I just focused on the most important thing at the moment—

"Yes."

Another sigh fell out of his mouth. He nodded toward the upstairs of the Big Barn.

"Up there. Under some of the rafters in the back."

I looked up at the barn, immediately feeling betrayed by

it. *Why would he do it in there?* Then I shot a look over at my decrepit old home. The old green paint was still visible from the backside. A lasting colorful look at the days of old.

"Wait. I thought it was in the house?"

Chief Allan shook his head, again rubbing the back of his scalp. *Nope...*

"There's enough shit that goes on inside there. I imagine he didn't want to take the risk..." He trailed off, silently thinking out the remainder of the thought.

"Of?" I asked.

"Of being interrupted."

"Jesus. Why... do you think he did it at all?" I asked, feeling like a confused child all over again. The Chief looked out at me, his eyes sinking into a deep pit of sadness.

"Who knows, Paul. I'm a strong believer in the idea that *things* happen for a reason. But this? What happened to Kyle? To..." He trailed off, fighting hard against tears. "I don't know what to believe anymore. If it was for a reason, I don't think I want to give that reason life."

"What do you mean?"

His hands danced around the side of his legs. He looked over at the big barn, the two windows watching us talk like Big Brother. You could tell it was a big bother.

"How 'bout we have this conversation somewhere else?" He practically begged.

I pulled my confused eyes away from the top floor of the big barn.

"I know a good place to get a patio margarita. It's within walking distance," I joked.

A painful grimace and a look in the direction of the restaurant. He muttered something under his breath before looking back at me and replying—

"Still on duty. How 'bout a coffee at the station?"

I looked the oversized Chief of Police over, curious about his intentions.

"Is this a voluntary coffee?"

A quick nod.

"Did y'all get rid of that old pot yet?" I winced.

Coffee is coffee, but the boys in blue around here kept the same old pot in rotation since the 1970s. That sort of age does a thing or two to the flavor. And a thing or two to your stomach.

"We got one of those fancy machines for Christmas a few years back. You put in the pod and voilà, magic cup of instant coffee. 48 flavor variety pack as well," he teased.

I took another long look around the old barns. I was here for Kyle... and to get answers about why he did what he did. A cup of Vanilla Cream flavored coffee isn't going to uncover that kind of thing just yet.

"I'll tell you what, Chief. I'll be around for a little while so... can we grab that cup another time?"

He gave a nod and put his hand out again. So, I took it and gave the old Chief my trademark smile. Then, he was on his way off the property.

"It was great bumping into you, Chip. I'll make sure *she* gets all locked up," I jested.

He stopped in his tracks and spun around. He sized every inch of me up... and took a deep breath.

"You can't lock up a virus, Paul. You can only do your best to contain the spread."

My firm stance started to sway. My eyes wandered across the ground and over to his boots. His composure had completely changed, and it was all because of *this* spot.

"You talk like this place is sick, like it's contagious or something," I said.

He took a step towards me—

"This place *is* sick. Always has been, always will be. It pollutes the mind... spreads through the entire body," he preached.

"Whoa, Chief. I lived here a long time... and I'm perfectly fine."

He let out a small laugh and pointed directly at my arm.

"Then why is your arm **black**, Paul?"

I looked down at my arm, and sure as hell, my skin was covered in black mold. It was oozing out from the fresh wound. I lifted my sleeve to see it spreading up to my shoulders. I tried to swat it off the surface of my skin, but the force knocked flakes of flesh off instead. I screamed out in pain and panic. There wasn't any tissue or muscle under the shedding skin.

It was just rotted wood, splintering out of my bones.

"**Help me!**" I screamed, holding my arm out to the burly man.

Chief Allan looked back at me confused... and scared out of his mind.

"It's just a little wound, Paul! Relax!"

I looked back down at my arm... and the small wound stared back at me. Barely a mark and the tiny bit of blood had already dried up. I ran my hand across my arm, testing it for mold, skin flakes, and rotted wood. *Nothing came off...*

I looked up at the Chief, who stared back with eyes filled with *told-you-so's.*

"Like I said, this place *is* sick. And it's spreading. I'll be ready for that coffee when you are."

He took off again... but I couldn't let him go without a plea.

"Hey... Chief."

He turned his head—

"Can you keep this little episode to yourself?"

He grinned.

"Paul, if I blabbed about all the shit I've seen out here, they would have never voted me Chief. I would've been thrown in the crazy ward YEARS ago. Besides, you're the one with the podcast. Seems like if either of us were going to talk about this place, it'd be **you**."

He gave a slight wave then disappeared into the overgrown trees. I sat there in dumb silence, not because I was embarrassed by what just happened in front of the Chief of

Police. I was just accosted by my dead friend in town not even an hour ago. Embarrassed seems to be the word of the day.

No, I sat there feeling stupid because Mr. Controversial Chief of Police just planted a brilliant seed. I came back home because Kyle killed himself on this property and nobody knows why. But to understand what happened to him, I needed to understand what happened to this place. What *could* happen to me... and I now knew the best way to do that.

Even if it was a terrible, horrible, no good, very bad idea.

Adam Benny is Missing –
Series Update
May 23rd, 2025

H ey there listeners... if there still are any.
It's Paul Early... and this is an update on the **Adam Benny is Missing** podcast... and us in general. I want to start out by saying we have heard you loud and clear. We've seen all the messages and comments and we're listening. Believe me, **we're listening**.

This will be the final update on **Adam Benny is Missing**. After this airs, feel free to unsubscribe from the series and our feed. The only real reason to keep it going is if Adam himself wanted to come on and talk about everything. But... he's made it very clear that he's not interested in doing that, so this is the last one. And honestly, I don't blame him.

I've unwittingly made his life hell. So, we're going to stand by his decision and not pressure him to appear. We plan on putting this whole saga behind us in hopes of helping Adam and this unfortunate situation out. And... to hopefully rebuild your trust as a listener. And a fan.

I can't say it enough... but I'm so incredibly sorry for how these circumstances played out. And how things continue to play out. I am back in my hometown for the foreseeable future *dealing with some personal issues... and the untimely death of one of my closest friends.*

*I don't expect many of you to feel bad for me... but it's been a tough loss. And it was under incredibly mysterious circumstances. Circumstances that I was prepared to ignore, but some people have convinced me that we should talk about it. That... **I** should talk about it. So, we're going to be launching something new soon.*

*And hopefully you will give us another chance and listen. Our goal with the **Adam Benny** podcast was to solve what I thought was a mystery... but our goal with this new podcast will be to figure out history and if it's repeating itself in tragic, horrific fashion. Plainly put, it's going to be scary shit. And I'm not really looking forward to diving into it all.*

*So, I'm inviting you to join us for the first episode of **8114** early next week. You can find a teaser for it soon. The series itself will be out wherever you listen to your podcasts. I don't know what kind of information it will unleash, but I promise the experience will be painful for **me**. And terrifying. And that should be good enough for **you** to listen.*

Stay safe and be well.

Bye for now.

Paul Early, signing off.

Chapter Six

The very idea of dedicating an entire new podcast series to 8 1 1 4 was daunting.

There's Chief Allan and his overwhelming sense of hate for that property. But to be honest, I got the feeling that he was already expecting me to pull something like this. Maybe not so soon, but he was expecting *something*. I also got the feeling that he wasn't really going to like it *very* much. He clearly already had his hands full keeping people out of the property, and a podcast focused on it could potentially bring more interest. And even more business to the curse-side Mexican restaurant he seemed to hate with a passion.

There's Matt and his family, not to mention Glenn. He has a particularly bone-chilling story about the night we all chose to play *Ghosts in the Graveyard*, with the graveyard being the barns. A rather ballsy and stupid decision looking back on it. *Note to self... maybe that should be an episode of the podcast. Hmmm.*

There are our other friends who will no doubt have to play a minor role in a podcast dedicated to the house they spent time in. Which... would be an interesting ask.

"Hey, I know we haven't talked in years, but will you

come on my new podcast and talk about that one night we saw ghostly figures watching us from the dark while we joked about girls and other ridiculous things? I'll buy you a beer!"

Ridiculous.

Truthfully, Kyle's surviving family is where the major issues start to arise with this new podcast. It might sound grim, but his wife Amber would be a *great* guest to have on and talk about Kyle.

Right.

Saying it back in my head, it does sound SUPER grim, but I don't mean it in the way it sounds. I mean, she could give him and his story some sort of life again. One that has meaning and hope, not one that stands over me in a parking lot, face innards leaking all over the fucking place.

There are his parents who I haven't talked to in ages... and would no doubt be against me making their dead son the star of a podcast. That's a big ask to expect a set of parents to not only accept that idea, but to accept that he died by sui—

Sigh.

It was still too hard to say. Even for me, so yeah, his parents would buy me a first-class ticket straight to hell. They might even offer to drop me off!

My final concern is what I would call the "Benny Base." The group of people that have spent every day since Adam Benny revealed the truth about his situation attempting to ruin *everything* about me. Slander, online campaigns and petitions, review bombing, and the occasional death threat.

And I get it, I do!

I get their anger and their desire to make me pay for my mistakes. But in a way, that would be the goal of the 8114 podcast... to make me pay. To make me suffer. To make me talk about the death of my best friend every single time I hit the "record" button. To dissect and look at every step of my life and figure out what happened, or what impacted it.

Maybe even *infected* it.

To figure out why I am the way I am. Why I've done the things that I've done.

8 1 1 4 will not be a laugh-a-minute debacle into underwear ads and piss-and-shit jokes. You won't hear me offering discount codes on stamps or dollar shave clubs. I won't be hawking audiobook discounts or mattresses. I'll be atoning and looking for forgiveness. For another shot to prove that I'm not a villain. At least that's the goal anyway. Hell, at the end of the day... I just might be the scoundrel everyone makes me out to be.

Who knows.

Maybe I'll be selling square space by episode five... if there even is one. I know Producer Rachel wouldn't hate that. It is her job to keep the show going by any means necessary. At this point, she has just spent most of her time trying to convince me to get *this* one going.

Aside from all the reasons I just listed, and told her personally, she still didn't seem to understand my reluctance. She simply replied with something like—

"You think it's going to piss a lot of people off. **So.** *People are already pissed-off at you. Like, a lot of them. If I were you, I'd just go on with my life because they'll still be mad at you regardless of what you do."*

And she was right. Come to think about it, Producer Rachel was usually right.

I thought back to the other night when Sheila Feela called me an asshole when I was just trying to have a beer. There was another time where I was having coffee, and someone threw their iced macchiato at me. People will still be mad. 8 1 1 4 podcast or not.

So, I'll let them be mad.

Maybe it will allow us to put the Adam Benny podcast out of its misery. And give my email and social media pages a rest. Give *me* a rest. Which would be good right about now... but there's no time.

I still needed a solid idea for the first episode of the

podcast. One would assume it would start with Kyle, but the podcast is called 8114, not *Kyle*. But... this is all happening because of *him*, even if it's about *everything* else. I need to remember that moving forward, regardless of my current feelings. He is just another piece of the puzzle that is this address.

This *sickness*.

It makes sense to start with the house. Like all these stories do. It's a haunting but you can't really get a grasp on that aspect until you know the house that's being haunted. Until you can see the location in your head. And sure, I don't know all of the history of 8114 but I know *my* history there.

Ideally, the first episode should be like the first ten minutes of a horror movie where a new family moves into an exciting new house. You know the scene I'm talking about, right? *The Amityville Horror, The Conjuring, Insidious, Sinister*, and so many more. It's an overdone trope but it was also my life. We did move into an exciting new house that turned into a real-life horror movie. So, I suppose that makes the most sense to start there.

But... it feels a little generic, doesn't it?

It feels like throwing in the towel before we even begin.

Here's the house.

Here's the spooky sounds.

Here's the ghosts.

Here's the struggle to get out.

Here's the scene where the family leaves and it's a hopeful ending.

Here's the scene where the house kills your best friend and tricks you to come back home because the things out there, **they want you back**.

My eyes went wide.

I had no idea where that last train of thought came from, but I wanted to move on from it as quick as possible. I wanted to... *itch my arm?* I looked down at the small wound I suffered out at 8114. *Was it sprouting something?*

I lowered my fingers and pulled whatever small weed was

now growing out of the contusion. The roots seemed to be never-ending, and for a moment, it felt like I was ripping my veins out with them. Finally, they were all out. The rootstock was completely black and oozed a dark liquid from the end. I threw it to the floor of the Airbnb and watched as it seeped into the cracks of the wood.

I looked back at the wound... black lines now splintered out from the ripped opening of my skin. *There was still something in there.* It made sense. My mom used to garden... and I remember something she told me about pulling weeds and why *we* shouldn't do it. You could expose dormant seeds that come up with the weed, resulting in a bigger spread once they germinate. The other fact she said was the exposed soil after pulling a weed is perfect soil to grow in. The less disturbance, the better. And here I am pulling them out of my skin.

Might as well call my personal horror movie The Germinating.

I walked over to the kitchen drawers and rifled through them until I found a pair of sharp grilling tongs. Setting my footing firm against the sink area, I placed my arm on the counter and used the edge of the tongs to pry... and flay my wound open.

The pain was too much to bear but I wanted to get a good idea of what the inside looked like. *Bad idea.* Like the corner of an old wall or ceiling, a severe mold infection was spreading *inside* of my skin. Green paint chipped off from the inside. I let the tongs open even more, taking some skin with them. I watched *it* spread before my eyes. Even worse, I could feel *it*. The scraping, the grappling. The growing pain.

Like the venom of a poisonous house, sinking its teeth into the flesh. **It was hungry.**

I looked at the end of the counter to see bottles of whiskey, vodka, and moonshine. I don't remember buying them but I'm glad I did. Another glance at my black mold-filled insides... then I grabbed the vodka. I pulled open the bottle and held it

over my tong spread skin. I glanced at the label and a realization struck me—

Vodka. Shit!

Matt should be the first episode.

He was our best friend. He spent a ton of time out at
8114. And maybe, just maybe, he would have some juicy
information about—*never mind.* I'm not going to finish that
thought. I finally had the perfect first episode for 8114. I just
needed to convince him. And... I will. I smiled in relief. Then,
like the goddamn fool I am, I poured the entire bottle into the
open wound and screamed until I blacked out.

8114 – An Introduction
May 24th, 2025

Hey there everyone.

It's your host Paul Early... and this is a teaser for *8114*. *A new true crime, real-life horror series from Fleas on Parade Productions.*

I know, I know. You're all wondering what exactly this is. What the hell is Paul Early doing **now**? *I don't really know... but I hope we're going to find out together. You the listener... and me the host.*

Let's start with the name.

I'm sure that some of the people who know me or know of me might recognize that number. It's the house I spent damn near twenty years of my life in. So, you could say this new podcast is about my life in that house. Or inspired by that house... and the property. But the truth is, we don't really know yet. We don't exactly know where this thing will go and that's scary as hell.

Why?

Because it's terrifying to look back on your life. Your mistakes and experiences. It's a weird thing to look back because you see everything so different. Life no longer has an exciting "the world is your oyster" filter. It's more like the world is an oyster shell, trying to trap you in, if you know what I mean? So, it's tough. And it gets even tougher when things happen like they have. I'll explain.

I'm back in my hometown due to the death of one of my best friends in the entire world. And I haven't been back home in about ten years. Not since my mom passed away. I'm seeing friends and other people I haven't seen in such a long, long time. But the one person I want to see most, I can't. And it's hard to wrap my head around that. It's hard to process the fact that I'll never see him alive again.

*And **why** I won't see him again.*

Kyle Robinson took his own life four days ago.

*I met him in middle school. Like, **truly** met him. We obviously went to school with each other our entire lives, but we weren't friends. That all changed when we hit seventh grade and we became inseparable. We loved basketball, rap music, and comic books. We always talked about making one together... but it never happened.*

Much like a lot of things we talked about.

Then we met our friends Matt Roberts and Glenn Sanders, and it was much of the same. Our duo became a foursome... and we spent as much time together as we could. We all got a job at the same fast-food restaurant. We all rode to school together.

*We were **best friends**. A crew.*

And that never changed, even after high school. Even after Matt went off to college. Kyle, Glenn, and I stayed around our hometown and got an apartment together. It was the party spot for a few years, but things must change eventually, you know? People need to grow up. So, I moved across the country to focus on my career, Glenn took a university job four states away, and Kyle stayed in our hometown.

He eventually married his on-again-off-again sweetheart from high school. They had two daughters... and life really seemed to be going well for him. Or at least I thought it was.

Until I received a frantic phone call from Matt earlier this week, begging me to come home as soon as I could. So, I jumped in my car and drove the eight-hour drive to meet him. It was in that meeting, over some random light beer, that Matt informed me that Kyle was dead.

That he had killed himself.

But... that didn't make sense. It still doesn't. Like I said, he had a family. They were happy. But that wasn't even the biggest bomb Matt dropped on me that night.

Kyle Robinson killed himself at my old house... at **8114**. A house he spent a big chunk of his life at. None of it made sense, but I suddenly started remembering all of these... **things** that happened in that house. All the death. And pain. And unexplainable events.

And the terror. People feared that place. And then what happened to Kyle... well—

I needed to figure out what was wrong with that house. That's what **this** is. Maybe it will help all of us here, who are so hurt and confused by Kyle's sudden death, to understand why he did what he did. And why he did it **where** he did it. That's the goal of this podcast.

To get to the truth, no matter what is uncovered. And I know, listen, **I know**. We've been down that path before, but this is different. This is... **something else**. This is the only thing I can give my friend now that he's dead.

You're probably asking yourself... is this a memorial podcast? True Crime? Is it a paranormal thing? Is it something... totally fucked up and unusual? I think it has a chance to be all those things... but we won't know until **we know**.

We're going to let **8114** take us where it wants to take us... good or bad. Lame or scary. Realistic or... farfetched. We're going to let this place tell its story. And I'm going to do my best to tell our story. To put you in that place and experience what we experienced. To fear what we feared. To try to understand what Kyle was going through in his last moments. In those final days.

*So, come home with me and join us for **8114**. It's going to be... killer.*

You know what's an odd feeling?

Asking one of your closest friends to be the first guest on a podcast about the death of your other best friend. It feels strange because that's exactly how his reaction made me feel. Like he was one of those classic *Real Ghostbusters* action figures who had the eyes that popped out of their skull. Like, I was out of my mind for even considering making Kyle, *sorry,* **8114**, the focus of a new podcast. Especially with the way the last one ended.

The Curse of Adam Benny continues...

"Don't you think it's a little... ghoulish?" he asked. His eyes weary and worn.

"Trying to figure out what happened to Kyle? How is that... ghoulish?"

He scratched the bottom of his scruffy chin. Then stretched his arms out into the sky, almost as if he was attempting to catch the sun and bring it closer. Like there was too much darkness around us.

"You know what I mean. Doing a podcast. Can't we figure it out... just like, on our own? Like the old days? And not make it a performative thing?" His eyes sunk, as if he knew it was a mean thing to say. That word—

Performative.

There it is again. One of my longest friends accusing me of "performing" for a podcast. Or performing for grief. Or attention. Or whatever the fuck people perform for these days. Everything is a performance, right? An act. Nobody is being honest about who they really are or their intentions.

At least, that's what *they* say.

"We all grieve in our own way, Matt. Plus, you know something isn't right."

"With you?" he grinned.

I let out a small laugh and gave a nod back.

"Well, that's obvious at this point," I said. "With that entire place."

He nodded, agreeing with that statement. Outside of my family and I, Matt probably spent the most time at 8114. Just a little more than Kyle, which is why I'm so determined. What if *he's* next? More importantly, and way more terrifying, but what if Kyle's corpse is right... and the house does want us back.

Wants *me* back.

Jesus.

It was all too much to think about. To even consider.

"I know you've seen things out there, experienced stuff that's hard to explain." I pleaded.

"But what if I just want to ignore it? I don't know if I can be a part of this... *thing*," he sunk his head even more. "I have a family, Paul."

"So did Kyle."

Matt looked up at me, unspooled tears suddenly surrounded the outlines of his eyes.

"Yeah. That's part of the reason he did what he did," he admitted. I leaned back, confused, and intrigued by the statement.

"What the hell do you mean by that?"

Matt scratched his entire face, then it morphed into him vigorously rubbing his shaved head. I watched as he grappled with where to unload his emotions and where to place his wandering hands. They moved down his face, then he clutched onto his neck.

He rocked back and forth, then looked me dead in my eyes—

"Do you remember the baby?" he asked.

"Kelly... *Emily*?" I formed my mouth into an awkward look, afraid that I once again messed up the name of Kyle's most recent child.

"It's Emily."

Judging by the worn-down look of Matt, I held in my celebratory reaction for *actually* knowing the name of Kyle's baby. Well, for knowing it with my *second guess*.

"Yeah. What about her?" I asked.

"Nothing. I'm not talking about Kyle's baby," he looked at me dead on.

For a moment, it felt like his black pupils had engulfed every aspect of his eyes. It felt like I was staring into a never-ending abyss of darkness. I worried it would start seeping out towards me, like a symbiote looking for a new host. Thankfully he finally blinked, allowing me to do the same.

"Then... what baby are you talking about, Matt?"

"The one from the barn," he said, in a matter-of-fact way. "Do you remember it?"

I cocked my head to the right and thought long and hard about any possible barn baby we encountered growing up. There were stray kittens and the occasional puppy. Tons of baby mice and possums. But that's all that my current memory could conjure up.

"I don't think I do," I said, admitting momentary defeat.

"Neither did I until he told me about it a week before he killed himself. That goddamn baby, man."

"What baby?!" I said, irritation washing over my entire body.

A slight, sinister grin spread across his face—

"*Up on the rafters, she needs no name. Let's give her back* to the ground with the hanging game. The hanging game for t=The Blackened Lady. She'll be so happy... about the hanging baby," his face sunk back into its normal, scared position. "**Do you remember now, Paul?**"

It felt like my heart stopped in its tracks. I forgot all about that terrifying sound of a baby crying in the distance... and the sound of it dropping and swinging into the wooden wall of the barn—**BANG!**

We only *kind of* saw it a few times... and that was more than enough for our teenage eyes. As a matter of fact, I think I blocked that horrible image from my memory. But the rhyme... we never heard that rhyme, so where the hell did it come from?

"I forgot all about that baby," I admitted.

"Me too. But not Kyle. He saw *it* every single day," he said, fighting the urge to tear up.

"What the hell was that... song?" I asked, creeped the hell out.

"*They* would sing it."

My mom ran a daycare out at the house... but that didn't seem like a song they would or *should* know. Still, I had to ask. "Who? Some of the daycare kids?"

"No, **The Women in the Light**. They would meet there... and sing it before the offering. *Up on the rafters, she needs no name. Let's give it back to the ground with the hanging game*," He stared back at me, zero emotions.

"I've never heard that before, Matt..."

Judging by the goosebumps all over my arms, I still wish I hadn't.

"Kyle heard it every night, right before he put Emily to bed." Matt sunk deep into his chair. "I don't really want to be on your podcast to talk about Kyle... and his death. But I'll come on and tell you what he told me about those women," He paused. "That horrible woman... and that goddamn baby."

I stared at Matt and his sad, red face. This was a man

carrying the weight of something sinister on his shoulders. Like it or not, I had to do my best to help lift it off...

"Then, that's what we'll do. That's episode one of **8114**."

He gave a nod... and his head took a small tilt to the right. The darkness spread across his pupils again.

"**Good**. She'll be so happy about *The Hanging Baby*."

Before I could even ask who *she* was, a layer of black mold grew out from under his eyelids... and his mouth opened into an unnaturally wide smile as an eerie groan spilled out. His mouth was wide enough for me to see all the way back to his tonsils. But they weren't there—

Only the grotesque outline of a hanging baby.

8114 – Episode One:
The Hanging Baby
May 27th, 2025

Hello... and welcome to the first episode of **8114**.

I'm your host Paul Early... and I'm here to guide **you** through my hometown and the house I grew up in. And the mystery that surrounds both. You may be asking me why you should care about either one. Or still even care about me... if you ever did. The answer is... you shouldn't. But I do ask, if you are here, that you consider caring about the situation.

Care about my friend Kyle.

And if you're asking who Kyle is, I implore you to go listen to the small introduction we shared a few days ago on this very feed. It'll give you a better insight into what we're doing here. What I'm trying to do here. And that's getting to the bottom of my best friend Kyle Robinson's mysterious death. And trying to find out why he took his own life at my old, abandoned house. A house he hadn't even been to in well over ten years. Just like me.

So, what happened? How did we get here? That's what I want to find out. Each episode will have a guest on to talk about Kyle, that house, or this town. We're going to figure this out.

Together.

And the best place to start is with Kyle and I's other best friend, Matt Roberts. Those two still saw each other and talked on a regular basis because they still lived here... in Pendleton. Their families grew up together. Hell, **they** grew up together. And now... we all find ourselves in this unbelievable situation of heartache and pain. Asking each other how this can be real. How did this even happen.

Well, the clue might be in one of the last conversations Matt and Kyle ever had. A week before Kyle took his own life, him and Matt met up for beers to talk and... well, it's pretty harrowing stuff. And it made the hair on my arms stand like crazy. Maybe it will have the same impact on **you**.

Here's my interview with Matt Roberts. Five days after the death of Kyle Robinson.

Paul: Hey Matt. I know we're all struggling here so I just wanted to say... thanks for doing this. And thanks for being the first guest on this new... adventure.

Matt: Uh huh.

Paul: You don't have to hold the microphone. You can just let it sit there in front of you. It should pick up everything just fine.

Matt: Everything?

Paul: Some movement, maybe chair squeaks. Some breathing. Nothing out of the ordinary.

Matt: What about other voices?

Paul: Only the two of ours...

Matt: If you say so.

Paul: *Right. So, let's start with the basics. How long did you know Kyle Robinson?*

Matt: *I thought we weren't going to talk about **him**.*

Paul: *I just want to give the listener an idea of your friendship.*

Matt: *We were friends... for over thirty years. Does that work for your listeners?*

Paul: *You good, bud? You seem a little... off.*

Matt: *I'm not good, Paul. This is weird... and awkward. And I already told you, I don't want to talk about Kyle. But you're pushing your shit on me—*

Paul: *We can move on, man.*

Matt: *I'm sorry... I just. It... it feels like there's something eating away at me from the inside ever since Kyle told me this story at Donnie's. Like it's dying to get out. And I don't know if it's what he said... or if it's the house—*

Paul: *The house?*

Matt: *Your house. **8114**. It's like you said. There's something wrong with that place.*

Paul: *Is that what Kyle told you that night?*

Matt: *He told me a lot of things. How it all started... but mostly how it was all going to end.*

Paul: *How it was all going to end? I don't follow.*

Matt: *All of it. All the way up to the last one.*

Paul: *The last what??*

Matt: *You'll find out eventually. Do you want to know who was haunting him?*

Paul: *Haunting?*

Matt: *Yes, Paul. What's with the questions? Are you suddenly skeptical about this? About them?*

Paul: *I just want to make sure things are clear for the listeners.*

Matt: *It all will be in the end.*

Paul: *Who did Kyle say was haunting him?*

Matt: *Tsk tsk. Not yet. You need to know about **them**... before you know about **her**.*

Paul: *Them who?*

Matt: *He called them **The Women of the Light**... but at first, they called themselves **The Saturday Club**. They wanted to progress forward with their social lives... and move out from just being wives and mothers. This was back in the 1800s or some shit. This town was an entirely different place. Dirt roads, everything like that. You know the deal.*

Paul: *That club is still around today...*

Matt: *In more ways than one...*

Paul: *When did they adopt the title of* **The Women of the Light?**

Matt: *A few years later. Some of them felt like they weren't progressing enough... and still being held back by the normal demands. So... they started spending some time in this secluded area out in a town founded by the Dale Family.*

Paul: *Wait... you mean Daleville?*

Matt: *Yep.*

Paul: *That means... wait, are you saying they started holding meetings out at Witch's Circle?*

Matt: *That's what it's known as now. Back then, they called it the "Circle of Light." Apparently... progress comes easier when some unexplainable shit starts happening in front of your eyes.*

Paul: *We spent a lot of time messing around out there.*

Matt: *We weren't the only ones. After these former members of The Saturday Club witnessed the phenomenon that they did, they became* **The Women of the Light**. *And be it that Daleville was a bit of a ride from Pendleton, they started holding meetings on the outskirts of town. Right off of Old 67.*

Paul: *Where?*

Matt: *Where do you think?* **8114.** *More specifically, inside that big barn of yours.*

Paul: *Jesus.*

Matt: *It gave them the privacy they needed to worship the Circle of Light... and all* **it** *stood for.*

Paul: *Which was what exactly?*

Matt: *The exact opposite of what you think something called the "Circle of Light" would be about.*

Paul: *Something demonic?*

Matt: *Whatever **it** was, it demanded... **things**. Pain, grief... blood. **The Women of the Light** became the women of inflicting chaos. Farm animals, pets, their own blood. And then... it wanted more.*

Paul: *...is that where the baby came from?*

Matt: *Sort of, but not how you think.*

Paul: *What happened?*

Matt: *The same thing that happens every time women start to stand on their own... **men**. Their husbands grew suspicious of all the rambling and disappearing in the middle of the night. The Women of the Light had a "leader" in a woman named Mary. She just had a baby... and as you can imagine... it wasn't to raise it. **It was to offer it**. But... all the other women were in different stages of pregnancy. Almost as if they planned to stagger sacrifices by giving the Circle of Light new blood every single month. Anyway, Mary climbed to the top of your rafters and tied the noose around the baby's neck. She looked down on a few of the pregnant Women of Light below her and sang—*

Up on the rafters, she needs no name. Let's give her back to the lord with the hanging game. The hanging game for the circle of light. It'll be so happy... we'll shine at night.

She kept repeating those lines as she propped the baby up, ready to drop it. But then... the husbands and a preacher burst into the barn, throwing the entire sacrifice off. Mary went to drop the baby... but her husband knew of her intentions and was hiding up top. He was able to grab his daughter and remove the noose. Mary snarled and gnashed her blackened teeth at her husband. Another man climbed onto the rafters and took the baby, allowing the husband to tie the noose around his wife. The Women of Light screamed below as he tightened the noose and stuffed the front of her dress with hay. He said nothing to her as he lit the dry grass in her chest, the flames spread, and he pushed her burning body off the rafters. They all watched as Mary burned to death, hanging above all of them. She never screamed. She never cried. She just sang and sang until she couldn't sing anymore. But the burning lyrics changed...

Up on the rafters, she needs no name. Let's give her back to the ground... with the hanging game. The hanging game... for The Blackened Lady. She'll be so happy... about the hanging baby...

*Mary fell silent and her body stopped moving, but she kept burning in front of the entire group. The Women of Light watched as Mary became **The Woman of Light** right before their eyes. And the husbands of death watched as she became **The Blackened Lady**. First Lady of the **Circle of Light**. Both names would cause more pain, grief, and suffering than Mary could have ever done alive.*

Paul: *How so?*

Matt: *The wax remains even if you blow out the candle, Paul. The Women of Light would eventually gift a baby to the Circle of Light on the grounds of 8114 a few months later. A young mother named Isabelle was able to commit the act without any interruption. And she again sang out the words of Mary.*

Up on the rafters, she needs no name. Let's give her back to the ground... with the hanging game. The hanging game... for The Blackened Lady. She'll be so happy about the hanging baby.

Before dropping the newborn baby from the rafters, she added an extra verse...

Down goes the hanging baby, for The Circle of Light.
For The Blackened Lady and anyone in her sight.
If she sees your baby, God bless your soul.
She'll be so happy with your baby, deep in a hole.

*Isabelle walked out of that barn that day knowing she gave birth to something... **evil**. Something that would dig its claws into that land and into the people of that place.*

Paul: *It's a great story, Matt. But what does all of that have to do with what happened to Kyle?*

Matt: *It's not a story. And it has everything to do with Kyle. That hanging baby haunted him his entire life... and he never knew what it meant. Or why he was chosen. But... he remembered that he was the first one to see that baby. He told us about it, but **we** never saw it.*

Paul: *We saw it.*

Matt: *I thought so as well... but we didn't. We only heard the loud bang against the wall of the barn. And we saw Kyle's face when he stumbled out of the barn. But we **never** saw it. We never saw that baby.*

Paul: *Shit, you might be right.*

Matt: *I know I'm right. And that night when he was telling me this story. He didn't know how to process it all. But he was like... a possessed man telling me that story. I know he was right about everything.*

Paul: *How?*

Matt: *Because of what happened the day he died. What Amber did.*

Paul: *What do you mean, Matt? What did his wife do?*

Matt: *...she hung their baby in their garage.*

Paul: *That's not true. That... can't be true. We would all know that!*

Matt: *No, we wouldn't. Nobody really knows... or, well... knew.* ***Your precious listeners, Paul.***

Paul: *Fuck. Fuck! H—how could you possibly know that happened?*

Matt: *I know all of it, Paul. I know what his screams sounded like when he found Amber... and poor Emily's body. And I know that Amber was singing that fucking song.* ***Both verses***.

Paul: *How?! Did he call you!?!*

Matt: *No...*

Paul: *How the hell do you know then?!?*

Matt: *Because a woman named Isabelle told me the next day. And I believed every word of what this... woman said to me.*

Paul: ...*Why?*

Matt: *Because she told me in my kid's room, right after I put them to bed.*

Paul: *You had to be imagining it, Matt.*

Matt: *No. It was all real. Especially what happened next...*

Paul: *Tell me...*

Matt: *You mean... **tell everyone***?

Paul: *Matt—*

Matt: *After she told me, Isabelle stepped to the side... and fuck, man. This Blackened Lady was standing behind her! And she was just, **oh god**, she was holding the hanging body of Emily the entire time. Letting her body... just sway back and forth. I couldn't take my eyes off her...*

Paul: *... did she say anything?*

Matt: *Who, The Blackened Lady?*

Paul: *Yeah...*

Matt: *No. She just pointed at my kids and smiled her cruel, burnt smile the entire time. **Like she was so happy...***

PART TWO
HOME

Chapter Eight

Old habits are hard to break, which might explain why I pulled up to the brand-new fire station thinking it was the local police station.

In the decade since I've been gone, the police moved their homebase right next to the public park. I completely spaced it and gave a polite wave to a few of the confused firemen outside who witnessed my temporary slip up. I didn't spend a lot of time at that old station... but probably more than most youths.

We got into a lot of *simple* trouble growing up. Toilet papering the "fancy" new neighborhoods out on the edge of town. Egging, forking, and other silly pranks. There were fights and other shenanigans that put my friends and I up close and personal with Officer, *sorry*, Chief Chip Allan.

We did a healthy amount of community service growing up, which meant a healthy dose of questions like *"When are you boys going to grow up?"* He stopped asking when we kept ripping our shirts off and screaming **"NEVER!"** all while thumping on our chests like a pack of Neanderthals.

Allan had a soft spot for us mostly because we weren't like the other troublemakers in town. We did dastardly teen stuff...

while some of the other teenagers were selling drugs, drinking, and breaking into small businesses. We were basically the cast of *The Sandlot,* and the others were just a bunch of Indiana clones of Ace Merrill from *Stand by Me.* But that was then.

We're now in the fucked up, ghastly timeline of Paul Early the Destroyer.

It's never a good feeling when you let down the adults in your life who thought so highly of you. And I know I let Chip down with everything that happened with Adam Benny. He'll probably never actually come out and say that, but I saw it in his face that day out by the barn. And I saw it in his face as I pulled into the parking lot of the brand-new police station.

His favorite group of kids were now either liars, going crazy, or dead. And I didn't know which one of us was better off with him at this point. But I was about to find out—

"You went to the fire station, didn't ya?" Allan asked, shaking his head in shame.

"Old habits, Chief."

He nodded, then spit a wad of chewing tobacco out on the sidewalk.

"Speaking of old habits... Pendle Hill had a factory ass-ton of toilet paper unloaded on it last night. You and Roberts wouldn't happen to know anything about that, would ya?" He asked, a full grin on every inch of his face.

"I have a good alibi. And an even better lawyer," I said, grinning at the old Chief, knowing damn well I didn't have either one.

He gave a small chuckle and tilted his head towards the station door.

"Ready for that coffee?"

"Like you're ready to be stuck out at that barn forever!" I joked, hoping that my comedic charm would take the edge off of both of us. It did **not**. His face scrunched up as he tightened his grip around the door handle. "Sorry, Chief. I'll workshop the new material. Coffee sounds great!"

He sighed—

"Probably should have sent you the coffee menu last night. It's goddamn out of control in here. Everyone thinks they are baristas now. Even Scott Rich is getting in on the act. Thinks he discovered the Crème Brulé or something," he said, shaking his head in frustration.

"I like Crème Brulé."

"Well, Paul. The big difference there is that you say it right. He brags about drinking Cream Brullies every shit ass day."

"I don't like those *near* as much," I said, getting an audible chuckle from him. With that, he pulled the door open, and I followed him into the police station.

Moments later, I stared out at the steam flowing over the top of my fresh cup of... something called Dark Magic Roast. *Appropriate for today's theme.* Chief Allan took a long sip of his coffee as he cleared off the top of his cluttered desk.

I caught a peek at a few open files, town documents, and possible donation forms. He muttered to himself as I looked around the interior of his office. Signs of a productive, fulfilled life littered the entire room.

Pictures of his family—*Wife, Son, Daughter*—interloped with pictures from his career and other framed accomplishments. A map of our town hung on the wall above him, which is a nice juxtaposition of duties. This seems to be the one and only place where the town watches over him, not the other way around.

He finally took a seat, which was quickly followed by a deep breath.

"So, I wasn't expecting you to come by so fast," he said, clearly already suspicious.

"Well, you made it sound so appealing."

A small *bullshit* chuckle... then he sipped from his mug. I took the opportunity to do the same. Another loud exhale then—

"What did you hear, Paul?" he asked, clearly dreading the answer.

The Chief seemed to be more scatterbrained today than he was out by the barn. There was a distance in his eyes that told me he was in a hundred different places right now. I wondered to myself what percentage of that hundred was him mentally walking the grounds of 8114.

And what percentage was too scared to go back.

"What makes you think I heard anything?"

"Because I've known you for over thirty years, Paul. You've never been so eager to get inside this office with me."

"This is technically my first time in this office," I said.

"Paul. What did you hear?" he asked again, the question gripping the air a little firmer this time. I cleared my throat—

"You said something out by the barn that stuck with me."

He nodded his head slowly, unsure of the direction I was about to take this coffee meeting. "Okay?"

"You mentioned that you believe things happen for a reason. But you didn't know what to believe about what happened to Kyle. You weren't just talking about his suicide, were you?"

Chief Allan furrowed his eyebrow at me and gave his mug of coffee a slight push away. He took a deep sigh and sat all the way back in his chair. He pinched the insides of his eyes with his fingers and looked over at the pictures of his family on the walls. I was staring at a man on an emotional roller coaster that wouldn't let him off.

"Who told you?" He asked, the weight of the world on his voice.

"Chief—"

He slammed the table with his fist, spilling some liquid out of both cups of coffee. Startled, I stared at the man glaring at me with stinging red eyes.

"Who fucking told you, Paul?"

I cleared my throat and rolled my shoulders. It felt like my heart was about to rip open my chest and crawl out across his desk. I swallowed my saliva... and then went for it—

"Did Amber kill their baby?"

Both palms covered his eyes... and he let out the kind of sound I've never heard leave his body. The kind of sound that shouldn't leave an adult body of any kind. Then, he pulled his hands down and tilted his head. I had to ask again.

"Did **she** do it??"

"Well, that's up for debate isn't it... *Paul*?" There was something about the way he said my name that just... haunted me.

"...Chief?" I asked, looking down at my cup of coffee and pulling it up to my mouth.

I glanced into the cup right before touching it to my lips and was horrified at the sight of clumps of mold floating on top. I lowered the cup back down to the desk, catching a glimpse of the Chief's outstretched palms.

They were also covered in black mold. From the tip of his fingers all the way to the base of his wrists. Active, contagious strains of corruption.

I took note of his entire body, now covered in the spreading decay. Tree limbs and vines were growing out of his gaping mouth. His cheeks started splitting like cracked wood... and then I saw the charred hand gripping onto his shoulder.

I looked up to see the horrifying face of what I assumed was The Blackened Lady. Cracked, charred skin, boiled eyes. Scorched strands of black hair. She was as wretched as wretched could be... and she was standing behind the Chief, staring directly at me. The sounds of a baby crying took over and I glanced to the side of the Chief's chair. The body of Emily swayed at The Blackened Lady's side.

Back.

Forth.

Back—**SLAM!!** Emily's body swayed right into the wall of the Chief's office.

I fell back in horror and tipped my cup of coffee over in the process. I averted my eyes to avoid whatever hellish fate The Blackened Lady, *or 8 1 1 4*, had in store for me.

"Jesus, Paul. What in the hell?!" Allan screamed out.

I peeked out from between my fingers to see Chief Allan standing up, looking at his coffee drenched pants.

"She was right there!" I said, pointing behind him. The Chief turned, and of course, saw an empty ass wall. *Goddamn it.* I was absolutely losing my shit. I shook my head, embarrassed about my second freak-out in front of Chief Allan in a matter of days. I was becoming the paranoid village idiot.

"I'm sorry, Chief. I thought I..."

Allan sighed and sat back down in his chair. He muttered a few frustrated words at his coffee-stained pants then sighed. He plucked some tissues and dabbed his legs.

"It's fine. A coffee spill is the least of my worries these days." He said, seemingly confirming something else was at play here. We both pulled our shit back together and I took a deep breath, making sure no one else was standing behind him.

"So...?" I asked, hoping he wouldn't confirm what Matt heard.

"It's true, Paul."

"Jesus Christ," I said, burying my head into my hands. It's one thing hearing it from a crazed, podcastian version of Matt, but hearing the Chief confirm it was so much worse. It *actually* happened.

Amber Robinson killed their baby.

And then Kyle killed himself.

"I just don't understa—JESUS, what about Autumn??" I sat up in my chair.

"She was staying with Kyle's parents. Still is." The Chief rubbed the back of his head. "It's a shit show, Paul."

"Where's Amber?" I asked.

"Over at the county lock up until we figure it all out. If we can..."

Get in line, Chief.

"Did she say anything?" I asked, hoping Amber Robinson was remorseful about what she did. He shook his head. *Nope.*

"She's just been singing and smiling. That's it." His face went crystal clear. "Paul, I need to know who told you about Amber. That news can't get out."

I thought about the podcast and how the news was most certainly out there in the world. Luckily, we didn't appear to have any listeners. Or anyone that cared. *Thanks, Adam Benny.*

"Matt told me, Chief."

His eyes darted around the room, and he scratched his head in confusion.

"Who the hell told him?!"

"You wouldn't believe me if I told you." I said, testing the *what the fuck is going on* waters with the Chief.

"Try me."

I gave a nod, sighed, and cleared my throat. Then I started to sing—

"Down goes the hanging baby, for The Circle of Light.

For The Blackened Lady and anyone in her sight.

If she sees your baby, God bless your soul.

She'll be so happy with your baby, deep in a hole."

I looked up to see the horrified face of the Chief.

"How do you know that song, Paul?"

"Is that what she's singing?" I asked.

He nodded up and down, scared as hell.

"Amber didn't... do that to Emily."

"We have proof." Allan said, making it known she wasn't getting out of anything. Maybe making it known that none of us were getting out of this like we thought we would.

"Sure, maybe. Proof that it was her hand that did it, but maybe not her mind. Or her soul."

He rubbed his chin.

"Are you trying to tell me she was possessed by... someone?" He asked, with the least amount of judgment I've ever seen in his eyes.

"Or *something*."

He sat back in his chair and looked me over.

"Okay, Paul. I'll hear you out."

"Under one condition," I said, catching him off guard.

"You're giving me the conditions to hear *you* out?" He asked, confused as hell. I nodded.

"Be the next guest on my podcast."

He shook his head, instantly irritated about my suggestion.

"Podcast?! Come on, Paul. Are you out of your fucking mind?"

"It's a different one, Chief."

"Different? How?" He asked, a *can you believe this shit* grin touching every inch of his face. I nodded.

"It's about the house. It's called... **8114**."

He looked up at me with a shocked face.

"You gotta be kidding me. So... you've decided to bring this town and your house into the trainwreck that is Paul Early radio shows?"

"It's not really radio, Chief."

"I don't give shit, Paul! What would your mom think about that?!"

I took a hard swallow and stared back, darting my eyes in a hundred different directions. It was hard to say what my mom would think about it... because she's been dead for ten years. Truth be told, I hadn't even thought about that aspect of this whole thing. What's that mean when you stop thinking about your dead loved ones? What's that say about you as a person?

"You don't know what it was like when we found her in there, Paul."

Found her.

I remember hearing about the state of the house. The state of her. An old woman running around naked in a home filled with clutter and trash. A hoarder without anything to hoard except for pain, sadness, and regret. She was alone and scared. Even though they were a cornfield away, the nearest neighbors got tired of hearing her scream throughout the night. Luckily, Pendleton's Finest arrived on the scene before anything... permanent happened. Sure, some of the officers chased her naked self into the barns and more. But they eventually found her... and helped her.

She died a few months later. A shiver went down my spine as I wondered if a piece of her was still out there running around those barns, screaming into the darkness.

"You're right. I don't... but I'm grateful you and your men were there, Chip. But this isn't about her."

"Doesn't matter, Paul. I'd be careful with that one... for multiple reasons. Christ, this Amber news better stay far away from that fucking thing, you hear me?"

I shook my head. *Too late, Chief.*

"It's not the same—it's not like... *Adam.*" I said, doing my best to reassure him of my intentions.

"You mean a shit storm?"

Yeah, that sounds about right.

"That's all over," I said. *Trying to believe it as hard as I said it...*

"Over? Paul, I was on the phone with the sheriff over at Greenville earlier this morning. It's not over, hell... the shit advisory is only going to pick up steam." He said, shaking his head in disbelief.

"What do you mean?"

"Carl Benny was arrested this morning."

"For what?"

The Chief took a deep, hard swallow—

"He killed Adam Benny's mother yesterday."

Chapter Nine

I don't want to sound like a broken record but none of this was supposed to happen.

If I could go back, I'd never follow through on the idea for that dumb podcast. I would just continue coasting through life on my laziness and charm. If I could go back, I would have never opened that old middle school yearbook.

I would have never wondered about what ever happened to Adam Benny.

And I would have never told the world he went missing.

But that's the thing about broken records, isn't it? They are a symbol of something that used to exist. That used to work properly... or serve a purpose. Like a favorite song. You can't listen to it on that vinyl anymore... but you can still see the title sitting on Side A or B. It's always there to remind you about how things used to be. And one section just plays over and over again.

So that's me. **Broken record Paul.**

Here to remind you that none of this was supposed to happen. Especially Adam Benny's mom being shot five times by her deranged ex-husband. It's hard to imagine what kind of anger and sadness it takes to shoot someone you used to know

—used to love—five times at point blank range. It's hard to wrap your head around something like that.

Especially when **you** are the reason it happened.

I wondered when the news about Sheila Benny would get out. When people would start spotting me out and about and start blaming me. Hell, it already seemed like the Greenville Police Department was willing to pin some of the responsibility on me. And Chief Allan didn't exactly sway my concern about potentially landing some sort of legal consequence.

I rattled off potential charges in my brain. *Involuntary manslaughter? Accessory to Murder? Fifteen years in the clink for giving out sensitive information?* I had no idea what they were thinking.

I had no idea what I was thinking.

This entire situation was fucking with every part of my head. I couldn't shake the Amber news. And I couldn't stop thinking about the fucking Blackened Lady. I needed to know more about everything. I needed to go back in time and see how everything was connected. See if there was any way to fix... *all of this.*

There was only one way to go back in time in Pendleton. And I'm not a religious person, so I didn't pray as I sat staring out at the town's historical museum. I just hoped with all of my power that I would learn *something* that could help the situation.

Maybe even help me.

The wooden building hadn't changed much since the *old* days. It still had a long wraparound porch and sat on the edge of the local waterfall and creek. Quilts still hung over the front steps and flowers stretched across the ground to form a welcome party to whomever was curious about the town and its past. Usually, that would be the elderly looking up old family connections or kids from the local elementary school out on a field trip.

I would imagine it's usually *not* a disgraced man being

haunted by the land he grew up on. Or maybe it is and I'm just jumping in a very long line of cursed locals.

I'll know soon enough.

I wondered to myself if whoever was inside the museum would think I was out of my fucking mind. Or at least in the process of signaling to turn on the crazy Ville turnpike. And maybe I was. Maybe I should think twice about telling someone that I've already seen the Chief morph into a moldy, dead-tree version of himself. Or that The Blackened Lady gleefully held the hanging body of Emily out in front of me. That I was accosted by my dead friend in a parking lot. That... my old house at 8114 was hungry and begging me to come back. That this entire town might be infected by *something* on that land.

That I decided to do another podcast about *all* of it.

I'm still not even sure how I feel about that, honestly. I probably should have taken the Amber reveal out of the first episode... but it was a MAJOR reveal. And it will be a MAJOR issue when people finally hear it. Deja vu shit. The Chief was right, the Adam podcast was a massive screw up. And now I'm back here digging up a bunch of painful, horrific memories for everyone.

I was still thinking about the Chief saying *be careful... for multiple reasons*. I'm still trying to figure out exactly what he meant by that. I get it from a sensitivity and legal standpoint with the Kyle situation. And I get it from a *personal* aspect. I haven't been able to shake the thought of my mother since Chip brought her up.

But aside from that, what other reasons could he mean?

The more imaginative side of my brain wants to immediately latch on to the idea of *this* town being secretly run from the shadows by some mysterious group. A "Greater Good!" type situation... but far more serious with less swans on the loose. Though... swans do occasionally get on the loose outside of their designated park. And maybe, *just maybe*, Chief Allan is nothing more than a proxy for them. I wonder if it's like when a new President is elected, and they get to discover all the top-secret information the government has been hiding.

Was the Chief informed of the town's dark history on his first *or* second day in office? Was The Blackened Lady at the welcome party? Or... maybe it's not like that at all and there isn't some secret society.

Maybe it's something even worse.

Maybe the "multiple reasons" means unearthing a long-abandoned evil that is currently hidden by overgrown trees and out-of-control grass. And it was waiting for the *right* moment to reclaim the property and those that soured it.

Or maybe he just meant I've already fucked enough things up and he didn't want me doing the same thing here in his town. *Our* town. I should be careful... for multiple reasons because it seemed like 8 1 1 4 was behind everything going on.

Kyle and Amber.

Matt's mind turning into paranoid, vanilla pudding.

The creepy shit I keep experiencing.

It's like the house is fucking with... *and* stalking me like a desperate ex. And not even in the *"give me one more chance"* sort of way. This stalker seems to be thinking more with the ***"we belong together forever and ever"*** mindset. Like I'm a child on a big wheel... and 8 1 1 4 is a pair of shiny twins. It was a thought I just couldn't overlook.

I took another deep breath as I watched an older woman slowly walk to the front doors of the museum. Crocheted purse hanging over one arm, key ring jingling in the other. Luckily, and unluckily for me, I knew her. Her name was Nancy Hart... and she had been the curator of the museum since before I was in elementary school.

Before unlocking the door, Nancy glanced over at the roaring waterfall the museum overlooked. Then a quick look in my direction... followed by a momentary stare. *I knew her... and she knew me.* A few seconds later, she was inside the doors, and I was frozen with anxiety.

I remember telling Producer Rachel about our little town museum once. I always laughed at her response to that little fact—

"That's how you know your hometown is messed up, Paul. There's a museum. You know what other town has museums dedicated to its history? **Salem**!"

I wasn't laughing anymore... and neither was she. Producer Rachel's throwaway comment now made me shudder in fear. Sure, this town didn't go on a massive witch hunt, but an angry mob did burn a woman alive, or so I'm told. And not to mention, I was currently parked directly across from a rock that pays tribute to a tree that hung three white men. And there's a distinct possibility that I'm a few moments away from discovering a lot more sinister shit that happened in this little historical town of ours.

Salem we were *not*... but death did seem to make itself at home around here. Nancy Hart would know all about it. Come to think of it, Nancy Hart would also most likely be willing to talk about it, not just with me, but with *everyone*.

There I go again. *Thinking about the podcast.*

Classic Paul move.

But... Classic Paul was right.

We were only a few days removed from the heart wrenching, terrifying interview with Matt and things weren't supposed to escalate that fast. The 8114 podcast went from zero to *what the fuck* in the first few minutes of that episode. I desperately needed to get another one in the can, so nobody lost interest. And for any listening traffic we might have. Especially since Chief Allan messed up my mental schedule by turning me down for an interview. I needed to lock in—

My phone suddenly buzzed with an alert. It was... a notification from the Adam Benny podcast feed. It was just one painfully blunt sentence: **Sheila Benny is dead, she was murdered.**

A massive ball of *fuck me* spit suddenly blocked every aspect of my throat.

The idea of the Benny podcast feed being updated with the news of Alice's deat—murder made me uneasy. For multiple reasons. I wasn't sure how that news would go over in the world yet... but I was damn sure it wouldn't be good.

For Producer Rachel.

For Adam.

For me.

I mean, shit. We were trying to build something new with 8114. Our goal, well *my* goal, was to put the Adam Benny situation behind us and leave it in the past. To bury that time capsule filled with fuck ups and lessons learned. And now someone is updating that feed... hoping to stir more shit up?

Why didn't Producer Rachel deactivate it?

This isn't going to help *anything* moving forward. I already know what the perception and public reaction would be. *I'm responsible.* And yeah, maybe... that's true.

Sheila Benny was alive and well until we put our podcast out into the world. She was alive and well when Episode Six of "Adam Benny is Missing" went live. And she was alive and well after we ended the podcast because it revealed the truth.

Her truth.

Now she's dead because of our podcast. So yeah, maybe I'm *not* the one that pulled the trigger. But I am most certainly the one who handed Carl Benny the gun. More alerts came ringing in. This time from Twitter and the other social media platforms.

Shit.

It's happening again.

I powered my phone off and sighed in frustration. I needed to get my mind straight before going in and talking to Nancy. I need to—**Ding!**

Another alert.

I looked over at my turned off phone. It was still black.

Another alert. And another.

They kept screaming out from the shut off device. I picked up the phone and touched the dead screen, just to make sure. Suddenly, a text alert from an unknown number came up. *How the...?*

I swiped it open with my nervous finger to see seven words waiting for me—

"This is all your fault, Paul Early."

I stared down at the phone, then I flipped it over and pulled out the SIM card just in case. I threw both on the passenger seat and stared out at the creek in front of me. A young couple stared back at me as they stood in the creek. There was something... off about them. Their swimsuits were like something out of the fifties. I leaned closer just as the girl-friend disappeared into the falls.

"Whoa!" The word escaped my mouth without even processing what had happened. The oblivious boyfriend turned to where she was standing, then turned his attention back to me. I pointed to the waterfall with heavy urgency. Instead of looking, the boyfriend pointed back at me... and his mouth slowly dropped open. Black water flowed out and drib-bled down his chin. Why wasn't he trying to save his girl-friend?? I had to help. I had to—**Ding!**

Another alert.

What. The. Fuck.

I shot a look into the passenger seat where my phone and its SIM card still sat. This was impossible. I looked back out into the water and the boyfriend was nowhere to be seen. Another text alert rang out and I had to look. I reclaimed the device from the passenger side and looked down at the screen. The same message was waiting twice, both in all caps this time.

"THIS IS ALL YOUR FAULT."
"THIS IS ALL YOUR FAULT."

Before I could even respond, a slideshow file was sent. **Jesus.** *How is this even happening right now?* My fingers hovered over the file for a few nervous seconds before clicking it open.

The first image was of a woman going about her shift at a

diner. The picture was clearly taken from the parking lot. I didn't recognize her or the diner. The second image was much closer to the restaurant. The woman was now behind the counter and appeared to be pouring coffee. The next image was a close-up of her pouring the coffee. So close in fact, I could read her name tag—

Sheila

I started to breathe heavier. What the fuck was I even seeing right now? I wanted to call Chief Allan. I wanted to vomit. I wanted to stop looking. I wanted to—

Look at the next picture.

I swiped the image away and went to the next one. It was an up close and personal picture of Alice Benny's gunned-down body. She was crumpled on the ground with four visible gunshot wounds to her torso area. The other visible wound was to the side of her face. It was completely blown off by a point blank range shot.

I couldn't believe what I was seeing. Who even had access to these? And why were they sending them to—

I stopped every thought I had as I looked closer at the horrific picture. Not for gruesome details... but because I'm pretty sure I just saw her body slightly move, but that's... *impossible?* I brought the device closer to my face and refused to blink. Her good, dead eye suddenly opened.

What the fuck.

It stared back at me, watching my every move. I closed my eyes and did my best to pinch out any confusion that might be hiding in the corners. A moment later, I reopened them to see my screen was once again pitch black. *Thank God.* It was all just my overactive—

"This is all your fault."

I turned to see **Sheila Benny's dead body sitting next to me in the passenger seat.**

I didn't have any time to react before she lunged at me in rage. She smashed my head against the driver's side window and unleashed a guttural scream directly into my ear. Her half-gone face pushed up against mine, mushing her facial insides onto my cheek.

"This is all your fault!!!"

I peered out of my window and saw two people right next to my car. I screamed for them to help until I realized that it was the boyfriend and girlfriend from the falls. Their skin was rotted and sagging, and they smiled and pointed as Sheila Benny continued to mush her motherly gore against my face.

I panicked and smashed my free hand on my car horn, turning my head away from the Sheila horror show to see Nancy Hart staring back in disbelief. I pulled my head off the window and looked over to see an empty passenger seat. And my phone still next to the SIM card. I looked out into the creek and there was no one there.

I shook my head and grabbed my phone, shoving the SIM card back in. After powering back up, I checked for the Sheila Benny files. They were nowhere to be found. None of it actually happened.

Shit...

N ancy Hart made her way across the rickety old
wooden floor of the small museum.

She adjusted every little thing that happened
to be out of place. She was tugging on the end of a hanging
quilt when my own floor-creaking feet broke the heavy silence
of the room. She turned and gave me a look, one that said she
was just a clear witness to my little front-seat solo shit show.
She turned her attention back to the quilt and lined it
perfectly to match the others hanging nearby.

"There's a reason why most museums have a no touching
policy. So, people like me don't have to spend the first twenty
minutes of every morning fixing all the things that the kids
touch."

I nodded, doing my best to seem understanding of her
daily struggle.

"Sounds like a real pain."

She sighed.

"It can be... but so is having the unrealistic expectation
that a bunch of elementary kids are going to keep their hands
to themselves. At least it was just the quilts this time. A few
weeks ago, the little germs got into the arrowheads."

She motioned to a collection of arrowheads in a glass box.
I glanced over at it to seem attentive.

"One kid had to get stitches," she snickered.

"Jesus," I said, shocked that the little bastard could even
hurt himself on one. I caught Nancy casting a somewhat irritated glance in my direction. I guess that meant she still went
to church. "Sorry 'bout that. Just seems like... there should be
systems in place to—"

"Prevent kids from stabbing themselves? Usually there
is... just like usually these teachers bring more chaperones
with them. It's hard getting people to care these days. Do
people still care about what you do, Mr. Early?"

Ask me again tomorrow.

I know she got a good look at me out in the parking lot, so
I shouldn't have been surprised that she dropped my last
name so easily. It's a small town so pretty much *everyone*
knows *everyone*. Still, it's been years since I've been back.
And I was a snot-nosed kid the last time I was standing inside
this building. Probably trying to get my snotty little hands in
that arrowhead box. So, either Nancy Hart has a great
memory, or she's been keeping up with the news.

I'm assuming it's both.

"You remember me?"

"It's my job to remember things, Paul."

I delivered a small smile and shook my head. "That's true
I guess."

She sized me up, an army of hand sewn quilts with
colorful patterns hung behind her, giving her a royalty feel.

"So, what are you here to see? Arrowheads? Quilts?
Pictures of when the waterfall was a swimming pool?"

"Actually, I'm here to see *you*."

I half expected her to jump back in shock, delivering a
Vivian Leigh-esque *"Great balls of fire. Why on Earth would you
want to see me?"* but she just delivered a silent nod and pointed
to her office. I followed her into the small space and took a seat.

Her collection of framed pictures was a mixture of family and historical photos. Knowing that Nancy Hart had lived here her entire life, some of her extended family members were probably in the historical frames as well. A few more quilts were folded and stacked neatly on an antique chair. She took a seat and stared back at me.

"I had a feeling I'd be seeing you, Paul."

Hell, now I was the one thinking about great balls of fire.

"How?"

A grin crept across her face, parting the Great Wrinkle Sea.

"Like I said, it's my job to remember things. And it's my job to know about this town and the people in it. I have a certain responsibility to keep up on those sorts of things. And I'm not exactly the most tech savvy person in the world but I have my internet set to notify me if certain words appear across the web. For instance, if the town of Pendleton is mentioned, I know about it. If any of the citizens are mentioned, I know. And... if any of the former residents happen to launch an ill approached podcast about our town, well—"

"You know about it."

She gave a nod.

"So... you can imagine my surprise when I found out our very own Paul Early decided he was going to do a podcast about our quiet little town."

Quiet might be the wrong word, Nanc.

"It's not really about the town though," I said, hoping it would ease her irritation.

"Isn't it though? It's about that old house of yours. That's in our town. You can't tell that story without *our* story, Paul. They are connected. Always have been."

Her face looked like it was ready to drop a big "TA-DA!" on me but her eyes looked different. Like they were hesitant to talk to me about anything involving that land or this town.

"Did you listen to it?"

Her head shifted to the right.

"I did. Interesting stuff."

Nancy Hart had a unique definition of the word interesting, especially when it came to a tragedy like this. At least one that differed from how I would define an *interesting* tragedy. For instance, I'm going to stick to the theme of Indiana history for this one. A tragedy that I find particularly *interesting* is the Hagenbeck-Wallace Circus train wreck that happened here in 1918.

That train had over four hundred performers on it and eighty-six of them were killed when an empty passenger train plowed into it. One hundred and twenty-seven others were injured. I know what you're thinking.

Why is that interesting?

It's interesting because the circus is meant to bring joy to families all over, but this particular circus would now be the reason for pain spread across eighty-something families. I don't know if that's more ironic than interesting. But I'm fascinated by the idea of a family of clowns burning to death in the destruction and whether their make-up applied dead faces were still smiling when the fire finally went out.

That's what makes the Hagenbeck-Wallace Circus train wreck an interesting tragedy.

But Nancy calling the first episode of 8114 *interesting* implies that she finds a mother killing her innocent child interesting. Far more interesting than a dead Strongman. Or trapeze artists. But I guess that's a tight rope to walk.

"What's so interesting about it?" I asked, afraid to hear her answer.

She sat back in her chair, giving me the impression that she could sense my irritation with her use of that word.

"I find the story your friend Matt told to be interesting, Mr. Early. Not the awful tragedy that happened to that family. And certainly not the horrific details you chose to reveal."

I cleared my throat and moved past the slight jab as quickly as possible.

"You mean... The Women of the Light?"

A slight nod.

"What do you know about them?" I asked, hoping for a little more than a nursery rhyme this time.

"That they deserve some of the blame for the nature of that property."

"Only some?"

"Before we go any further, let me ask you something. Do you believe in curses, Paul?"

Curse is a funny word to throw around. There's obviously the Kennedy curse... and *Halloween 6: The Curse of Michael Myers.* There's the Salem curse. Tutankhamun. The Macbeth curse. Hell, there's even the curse of the Bambino. I could go on and on about "famous" curses but to ask me if I believe in *actual* curses?

I would have said no before we started the Adam Benny podcast.

Now? I think I'm cursed to deal with that situation every single day until I die. I still hadn't even turned my phone back on since the Sheila Benny news got out because I was so afraid of what was happening on it. *Does that count as a curse?*

"Depends on how you describe it," I grinned, even delivering a slight shrug with it.

"There have always been people in this town that have thought that land you grew up on was cursed," she said. A stern eye staring back at me.

"Are you one of them?" I asked, genuinely curious.

She leaned up, placing her elbows on the desk.

"I have my personal feelings but I'm curious what you think, Paul."

What do I think?

Hmmm.

I think there has been a lot of unexplained shit that has

happened at 8114. Like something is always there but it's not exactly *good*. Almost like a parasite waiting for the next carrier to enter. What exactly are the people that come in contact with that place carrying once they leave?

"I think... that places can be sick. They can be contagious. That if a property has seen enough darkness, it can spread. If you spend enough time there, then yeah, that darkness can get to you. Sort of like a curse."

She nodded.

"That property was built on darkness, Paul. And that's how it will stay."

I stared back at Nancy, watching her every move. I realized that I have only ever known her as a quiet-lifer who kept to herself and kept the town alive. Now she's playing the sort of role in a horror movie where the expert or professor cracks the case and tells the audience about the mysterious evil. I realized that I was about to learn more about my mysterious evil than I ever wanted to. And I didn't even bring any fucking popcorn.

"Would you want to be a guest on the show?"

"Of course... but we're not quite done here."

I looked back at her, expecting to see The Blackened Lady watching me or something else hovering. Maybe an explosion of spores and vines. But it was just plain ole Nancy.

"What was happening to you out there in the car?"

It would be hard to find the right way to explain that Adam Benny's corpse mom had somehow... jumped into my car from my dead phone and started attacking me. And two ghastly teens were taunting me about it. Again, it was hard to explain any of the shit that's been happening to me lately.

"Allergy attack."

A doubtful nod response—

"Are you familiar with the number fourteen, Paul?"

"Yes. It's right after thirteen. And right before fifteen," I say, grinning from ear to ear. Nancy on the other hand was *not* grinning. If anything, her face was worried. Not for herself, but for *me*.

"*You* should take this more serious."

I've heard that my entire life. *Is everything a joke to you? Will you be serious for one minute?* Now that I think about it, sarcasm and not taking *anything* serious is my gift.

Or my curse.

I put on the best straight face I could find. "Okay, familiar in what way?"

"What some people think the number fourteen represents."

I offered up an honest *I have no idea* shrug because I truly had no idea. People are always trying to give things meaning. *Seriously.* Give them enough room, and people will think an oddly shaped Cheeto represents Jesus Christ making love to Lady Gaga.

"When The Egyptian God Osiris was murdered, his killer cut his body into fourteen different pieces. His wife, Isis, found all the remnants and gave him, and his body parts, a proper burial. So, the number fourteen is associated with death and resurrection."

"So, which God was cut into eighty-one pieces?" Sure, I probably should have delivered that with a little less sarcasm. And judging by Nancy's face, she would have appreciated that.

"I will only ask one more time, Paul. I need you to take this seriously... for multiple reasons."

Shit.

There's that "multiple reasons" thing again. I wondered if Nancy Hart and Chief Allan had been comparing notes. But I don't dare ask—

"I'm sorry, it's just... what exactly are you getting at here, Nancy?"

"That fourteen represents death and resurrection. And that property has seen a lot of death. And resurrection."

"Are you talking about Kyle?"

She tilted her head and looked me up and down.

"I meant Mary—"

"The Blackened Lady."

She nodded, but clearly hated that nickname.

"There are so many others. There is a curse on that land, always has been."

"How do you know?"

"Again, it's my job to know about the history of this town. I can try and tell you multiple stories about that property and the land you grew up on that will no doubt convince you of that curse, Paul."

"Try?" I said back, confused by the statement.

"As in... if *it* lets me."

I assumed the *it* was the house or the property. And... I ignored all desire to respond with something like *what if you ask nicely*. What can I say? I'm learning.

"Then that's what we'll do for the podcast. How's Thursday sound? I have Kyle's funeral tomorrow." I realized I mentioned his funeral far too casual as she stood up from her chair and nodded.

"There's a reason you're here, Paul. And it's not because of that awful thing that happened to your friend," she paused. "The things out there, they want you back."

I took a deep, hard swallow. A chill traveled up and down my spine. *The things out here, they want you back.* That's the same thing Kyle said to me in the voicemail.

"How... how did you know he said that to me?"

Nancy looked at me in shock.

"Excuse me?"

"What you just said. *The things out there, they want you back.* That's what Dead Kyle said to me the other day."

"I didn't say that, Paul. I said I'm glad to see you back."

Goddammit.

At least I didn't dump coffee this time.

"Sorry. I... misheard. So, Thursday?"

She gave a nod and slight wave goodbye. I shook my head

and made my way to the door. Hoping to get out of the museum without any more surprises.

"Oh, Paul?"

I spun around.

"Yeah?"

"I know you think that it's just a number... but it's more than that."

"Like fate or something?"

She gave a wry smile.

"Or *something*. Do me a favor and read this when you have the time."

She handed me a small piece of paper that I promptly shoved in my pocket.

"Sure..."

I walked out of the office and stopped next to the hanging row of quilts. I decided to give Nancy's little piece of paper a look. I unfolded it to see what appeared to be an unanswered math problem on it. And my skin turned as pale as could be—

$8 + 1 + 1 + 4 =$

Chapter Eleven

F unerals aren't exactly my favorite pastime.

I'm not suggesting there are people out there who LOVE going to these things. Come on. They're usually filled with sad people and bad food. But I think there are some people who enjoy this sort of thing, as sick as that might sound. Or maybe that doesn't sound sick at all. There are people out there who buy random used underwear from strangers online. So... *sick* is a relative term.

I personally never do well at them.

Some would say I just don't do well at anything that needs "my emotions" to be present. I on the other hand, would say that I'm just very good at handling my feelings. *Did you hear that?* That was the sound of multiple exes going full Tony Clifton and crying out *bullshit bullshit bullshit* from the shadows.

I remember being at a funeral for my Great Aunt and everyone was heartbroken. I watched my Great Uncle refuse to let go of her dead hand for over an hour. A lot of people thought that was romantic.

Me? I thought it was a little weird and possessive. Not to mention a little rude since he stood there, blocking everyone else from saying their final goodbyes. My mom said she understood him though. They were married for over thirty years, and he just didn't know how to go on in life without her.

"Sometimes the living just can't let go of the dead," she told me.

I wonder what my mom would say about the dead not being able to let go of the living. I'd ask her why everyone was paying respects to the closed casket of Kyle while his dead version stared at me from one of the funeral home doorways.

Again, funerals aren't my favorite thing. Especially when the person you're burying is waving at you to follow him—*it?* – into a dark room.

I made my way over to the area where Dead Kyle was waiting. As I made my first steps into the big room, it felt like everyone stopped what they were doing and just watched my every move. Faces I hadn't seen in years judged every inch of floor that my scuffed dress shoes touched.

Other more friendly faces gave slight nods and "I'm so sorry" looks.

I caught a glimpse of a grieving pair of adults near the casket. It was Kyle's parents, heads down and broken hearts fully in each other's hands. There was no sign of Autumn anywhere which was *probably* a good thing. They didn't notice me... which was also a good thing. I kept my distance. I'm sure we'll talk later in the day. *In fact, I know we will.* The first episode of 8114 had already been out for a few days. They were going to find out... but right now? My focus was solely on their dead son, who was currently staring at his parents with gutted—

"Paul?"

I turned to see Megan Carey, my high school girlfriend, staring back at me. She looked great, *I mean*, she looked great given the circumstances. *Am I even allowed to think that sort of thing anymore?* I glanced back at Kyle. His dead face grew slightly irritated by the momentary interruption. I returned my gaze to Megan—

"Hey!" I pulled back on my excitement to see her. "Hey."

"How are you doing?" She asked with genuine concern spilling out of her lips.

How was I doing.

I was here to bury my oldest friend. But I was also here to apparently talk to my oldest friend who—yep, was still standing in that doorway, dead and waiting. I was suddenly starting to feel like I was bitten by an American werewolf I just didn't remember.

I looked back at Megan. "Oh, you know me."

She smiled.

"I do... which means you're probably burying all your emotions deep down inside. You'll let them out later after a few drinks?"

Yes.

No.

Yes?

"Come on, Megan. You of all people should know I don't have *any* emotions."

Her face sunk a little. She didn't even have to say *"I know"* because it was written across her face in big bold letters.

"That was a joke," I said, trying to ease the uncomfortable situation.

"Right. Another Paul Early trademark. Jokes at the *worst* possible time."

Again, it takes a certain skill to be able to give jokes a home anytime, *anywhere*. It probably takes even more skill to put up with someone like me for years. Especially "high school" me.

Also, clearly "current day" me as well.

I gave my neck an awkward scratch and looked over. She really did look great.

"Well, enough about *me*. How are you doing?"

Her head swayed and she looked the room over. She couldn't find any words until—

"This whole thing is... hard. There's the fact that Kyle was such a big part of your life which meant he was a big part of my life. But then... Autumn and Sarah are best friends so—"

"Sarah?"

Disappointment filled Megan's face as she bit the inside of her lip.

"That's my oldest daughter, Paul."

"Right! Sarah! Sorry, I don't know what I was thinking. Everything has turned my brain into..."

She put her hand on my wrist. "It's okay. You have a lot on your plate."

I looked down at her hand. Her touch was still as soft as I remember. Her tone just as kind. I went to touch it back, but she pulled it away—

"So, oldest daughter Sarah. Next in line is... Grace, right?"

She gave a nod and tilted her head. *And then who?* I stared back, blank-faced and confused. I thought she only had two kids.

I swore she only had two kids.

"I, umm, thought there was just Sarah and Grace?"

I felt her once again put her hand on my wrist.

"There was a third one. But..."

But.

I looked down at my wrist. A burnt, crispy hand was now stroking my wrist. I looked over into the darkened doorway. Dead Kyle was no longer there. I ignored both extremely haunting situations and cleared my throat. "But?"

I closed my eyes, then reopened them to make sure I was seeing Megan's face and not some hideous Ed and Lorraine ghoul.

It was just Megan.

Only Megan.

"But we... lost her a few days after..." We shared a moment of uncomfortable silence that strayed a little too close to home. She took a deep breath and put on a fake smile. "We don't need to talk about that here though."

Here.

Right. **Kyle's funeral.** I looked back at Megan. *We.* Right.

"Where is Nick?"

She replied with the sort of look that told me that was a long story.

"Maybe we shouldn't talk about *that* here either."

I gave a nod back. "Sure, totally. None of my business at all."

Some crying pulled my attention away, so I glanced over in the direction of Kyle's casket. An old girlfriend was crying over the closed mahogany wood. Even stranger, Dead Kyle was standing right next to her. He was just staring at her crying over his dead body... *as* a dead body. Then, he looked at me and motioned for me to join him. His face told me he was no longer willing to wait for my catch-up session with Megan to end.

"So, listen. I gotta go take care of something but—"

"Yeah, you should go. Want to meet up for a drink after all of this?"

I stared back at Megan. I wanted to say no with every ounce of my body... but instead a big fat **YES** spilled out from my lips. *Crap.*

"Donnie's?"

"I mean, is there even another option in this godforsaken town?"

She cracked a small grin, then quickly morphed it back into a straight face. Butterflies filled my stomach at the thought of having a drink, *or drinks*, with Megan after all of this. I never knew how much I missed her until this very moment. What a strange, shitty thing to say at my best friend's funeral. *Where was that Julia Roberts sequel?*

Megan gave the sort of nod that told me she was excited about having a drink with me. A nervous feeling crept under my skin. Not like the dancing butterflies from a few seconds ago. These were the kind of nerves infected by the rot of a certain property.

I was beginning to worry that I might rope her into all my bullshit. Then again, we were together for over four years. She spent a lot of time at 8114. Knowing what little I know about that place now; she's most likely *already* roped into my bullshit.

I touched the inside of her arm and gave a *"See you later"* look, then made my way through the rest of the room. More eyes watched my every move, but I was still mostly just focused on the dead eyes of Kyle. And trying to remember Megan's drink of choice. I realized as soon as I walked away to follow the corpse of Kyle, that I had no idea what Megan liked to drink as an adult.

Sure, we had drinks during our relationship, but they were of the *you guys are underage, so you get whatever the hell you get* variety. A lot of Smirnoff Ice and wine coolers. I pity the version of Paul Early that shows up at Donnie's Place tonight and orders the woman he wanted to marry a fucking Smirnoff Ice.

Maybe I should ask Dead Kyle if he remembers.

A grim laugh spilled out of my mouth as I followed him down into the basement area where the funeral home prepped the bodies. It felt weird being in the place he was just prepped. Well, not just weird. It felt ominous. Like more eyes were on me down here than up ther—

"Paul."

I spun around to see Dead Kyle standing in front of me. My words were stuck in my throat.

"We always wondered if Tiffany would cry when I died."

I cleared my throat and gave an awkward nod to the bloody human carcass standing in front of me.

"There's, uh, there's a lot of people crying up there, man. People are pretty... fucked up about this whole thing."

Kyle titled his head a touch. *This whole thing*.

"Oh, you mean... *this?*"

I watched as Dead Kyle put his bloated, gore-filled face on display for me. He clicked his tongue and shrugged.

"Some things are just out of your hands."

I looked down at his hands. **They were covered in black mold.**

"Whose hands were they in, Kyle?" I asked, afraid to get the answer. He grinned, then started walking around the confined space.

"Are you afraid of me, Paul?"

No.

Yes?

Hell yes.

"I'm afraid of what happened to you."

He stopped pacing and made a sad face in my direction. "I was hoping Autumn would be here. I just wanted to see her one more time."

Christ. I might be a cold-hearted bastard, but that comment might break me. I cleared my throat and held back tears.

"Can't you just go see her?"

"That's not how *this* works, Paul."

"What is *this* exactly?" I asked, desperate to learn even the slightest of inside information.

"It's fate. It's where we all belong. With the things out there."

Out there.

At 8114.

"Is *she* behind all of this?"

Kyle grinned, accidentally letting a little bit of gore spill out of his mouth.

"She belongs out there as well. But *this* is not her. It's the ground. It's that entire property. It's you. It's me. It's the ones that will soon join us. It's all of it."

I stared back—

"The ones that will soon join us? Are more people going to..."

Before I could even finish the question, he smiled and nodded. *Yes.*

"So, tell me how to help. How to... stop it."

An eerie, sinister laugh tumbled out of his mouth. *Yep.* I was *now* officially afraid of Kyle.

"There is no stopping this. There is no helping. There is just darkness. You need to know that, Paul."

I shook my head and glared at my old friend.

"**Bullshit.** You're haunting me. That means you have a purpose!"

"My purpose is to tell you there is *no hope.* **No way out.** You'll be with the things out there soon enough. There's nothing after the last one. Nothing but darkness"

"Hey!"

I spun around to see one of the funeral home employees staring back at me with a confused look. "You can't be down here."

I wiped my eyes and nodded. "Sorry."

Then, I hightailed it up the stairs and hustled through the crowded room of grievers. My destination was the front door, but two hands stopped my momentum. I turned to see Kyle's **angry dad** staring back at me. Kyle's mom stood behind him, tears pouring from her eyes.

"How dare you come here."

"What? Why... wouldn't I?"

"Our son has only been gone a few days... and you're making a show about him? About our dead granddaughter?"

I looked out at the onlookers. Sadness, rage, and embarrassment waited. Dead Kyle watched the entire show as he stood next to his casket, hovering over his lifeless body.

"It's not like that. It's—"

Before I could finish the statement, Kyle's dad punched me in the face, knocking me to the ground. A few random people in the crowd pulled him away as I jumped to my feet and wiped the fresh blood from my lip. I wanted to say *something*. Hell, I wanted to apologize. But all I could do was turn and head for the door.

That's when I saw the pale face of Matt staring back at me from the back of the room. No emotions, no *anything*. Like he didn't even know who I was. Or that The Blackened Lady was standing directly behind him with her hand clamped down on his shoulder.

Chapter Twelve

I t felt strange to be back at Donnie's Place so soon.
The same spot where I found out about Kyle's suicide a little more than a week ago. Now I'm back... right after Kyle's funeral. Well, Kyle's viewing, even though there was no Kyle to view. It was made clear by the punch to the face that I was *not* welcome at the actual service. Part of me wanted to tell all of them that I still get to talk to him. Rub it in their smug, judgmental faces that I still get to see him. That I'm better than *them* because he chose me.

Chose me.

Kyle said this entire situation was fate. That we all belong out there. Did he mean this entire town or just my family and friends? Or was it just me? And why couldn't he go see Autumn? I'm not a paranormal expert, but ghosts should be able to go wherever they please. Go see whoever the hell they want to. A dead dad should be able to see his only surviving daughter, right?

I should have asked him more questions. I should have asked about Matt and how long he has. My heartbreaking guess is not long since The Blackened Lady has latched onto him like a parasite. How long until his kids are dead? How long until I'm getting punched in the face at his memorial service?

How long until I'm talking to *his* corpse? How long until more people die? And who will it be? It was all so overwhelming to think about. The ding of a new email sounded out from my phone, thankfully breaking my Devon Sawa, *Final Destination*-esque investigation.

I glanced down at the screen to see that I had a new message from Producer Rachel. The brief subject line was a mix of exclamation and question marks. Maybe she uncovered something about the property. Or heard some new developments on the Adam Benny front. Whatever it was, it could wait until *after* I had drinks with Megan.

Drinks.

Right.

I looked down at the table and remembered the beer I ordered. I lifted the pint glass to my mouth, letting the cold rim soothe my busted lip. It hurt like hell. Physically and... emotionally. Kyle's dad *actually* punched me in front of all of those people.

It was hard to think about.

I had only seen that man angry a few times in my life. Once when Kyle and I took his car out joy riding in high school while we were on summer break. He couldn't take his rage out on me, but he sure took it out on Kyle. The other time involved the aftermath of a party we threw and forgot to clean up. But again, he couldn't take it out on me because I wasn't his kid.

And I was underage.

I guess it all caught up to me tonight. *Everything* seemed to be catching up to me lately. *How much more would?* I glanced out at the Donnie's crowd, hoping everyone was too busy in their own drinking worlds to notice me there. And that was the case for the most part. People mingled and laughed, ordered drinks and food. They danced to the Gaga-blaring jukebox and sang along with the catchy pop music.

I noticed one person not partaking in any of it. No drinking. No singing. He just stared at me from a dark corner near the front of the bar. The only light shining down on him was from a generic neon sign that read "**See you later!**" I leaned over the table, trying to get a better look at the man staring me down. I had zero luck, and he clearly had zero intention of looking away, so I pulled myself out of the booth to get a closer look.

And by closer look, I meant I was going to ask him just *what the fuck his proble—*

"Paul?"

I looked away from the Watcher to see Megan staring back with a curious face.

"Where you off to?"

I cleared my throat and cast a brief look back into the front corner and the Watcher was suddenly gone. *See you later indeed.* I gave her a sly grin and nodded at the bar—

"I was going to get you a drink... but I realized I don't really know what you like. Unless it's still Smirnoff Ice?"

She grinned and gave a slight shake of her head.

"Sure isn't. I also don't really listen to the Backstreet Boys anymore either if that helps."

"That's a huge help. I mean, it's slightly late because I just bought us tickets to their upcoming concert at Deer Creek or whatever it's called now."

"Oh really? They're coming *here*?"

"Yeah! You didn't know? Backstreet's back!"

And just like we were right back in high school, Megan unleashed her loud, adorable laugh in the back of Donnie's Place. It felt great to hear it. It felt even better to see it up close and personal. I truly missed her and all it took for me to realize that was... *all this 8114 bullshit.* All of this—

"Jameson and Ginger, please."

I gave the kind of nod that told her I would have *never* guessed that drink in a million years. Then, I left for the bar top and glanced at the front corner of Donnie's Place. The

Watcher was still gone... and oddly enough, the neon "**See You Later!**" sign was now out.

After returning with her drink and a new beer for myself, Megan and I spent the next hour or so playing catch up. We asked each other the pre-loaded polite cues like... *How is your family? How's work? You still talk to anyone from school?* Then slowly segued into more serious life catching up.

She asked why I was still single and the only thing I could think of to reply with was *because I'm me*. Even though what I really wanted to say was *because you are married*. I didn't know if that was true or not. We had a great relationship back in the day, but we were also kids. High school sweethearts that... started growing up. Started drifting apart. Started making mistakes... that would turn into lifelong regrets. Maybe even into bitterness.

I don't know who Megan is now. And I certainly don't know who the hell I am anymore. What the hell I'm doing. I certainly don't know if she would even be interested in current day Paul. *Is anybody??* But then again, she was the same Megan, just older.

And still so goddamn pretty.

I asked her about Nick and why he wasn't around for Kyle's funeral. That's when our personal Donnie's booth boat started to take on water.

"Because... we're getting a divorce."

She delivered the news just as I started to take a drink of my beer, so half of the sip spilled out of my lips. I wiped the ale mess away and set my glass down, staring back at her in shock.

"I'm sorry, what?"

"Divorce. It's what happens when a marriage stops working." She winked and took a sip out of her refilled Jameson mix.

"That's... awful. I'm so sorry to hear that." I stared back, my genuine words feeling like they didn't land with the intended effect. And I don't blame her. Megan knew that I still had *some* feelings for her. Or at least, she knew I still thought about her and looked at her from time to time. There was an accidental like of one of her recent Instagram pictures of her on vacation in a bathing suit.

"Are you *actually* sorry to hear that?"

I leaned back and rotated my glass of beer. "I am. How are the girls doing with everything?" She rocked her head back and forth.

"They're having a tough time, but we'll all get through it together. That's the goal anyway, to make sure we're together... no matter what. I think I would die if I didn't always have them."

I took a deep breath and watched as she stared into her drink. There was a moment where her eyes looked lost, like they were deep in thought. As if, she was in another place. Maybe back in high school... with me. *Or maybe not.* She looked up and snapped out of the momentary trance, forming a *yikes* look.

"Sorry about that. Sometimes I just—"

"...like to get dark as fuck? That was some grim shit right there, Megan Carey."

She wiped the corner of her eyes and took a deep breath. I hadn't even noticed the tears—

"Okay, I'm sorry."

"No, no, no. Don't be. That can't be easy for you and the girls," I said, before forming a big grin. "But... I do hope it's been hard for Nick."

She let out a small laugh and shook her head. "It was his choice."

"**Idiot.**"

It just came out. And before I could recover, she dropped her jaw and let a small, flattered laugh fall out. "Tell me how you really feel, Paul."

"Sorry, no offense to your soon to be ex-husband. How soon by the way?"

She rolled her eyes and waved her hand for me to keep going so I did—

"Right. It just seems like a bad move for him. He's not going to do any better than... *you*. And he's going to have to split all his shit. Doesn't he collect toy cars or something? Oh, and he'll have to share time with the girls. He could just suck it up and come home to you every night."

She shook her head at me, biting the inside of her lips.

"First of all, they are called *Hot Wheels*. And some of them are worth a lot of money."

"Which means... you now get half of that Hot Wheel money."

"Those are off the table. He's letting me keep the Beanie Babies."

I hid my *is this real or not* look behind another drink of beer. I'm glad I did since she burst into laughter a few seconds later.

"Nick doesn't collect *Hot Wheels*, Paul. Model kit cars. They were passed down from his dad. And he got rid of most of them when the girls were born."

"Well, that's good. I was starting to think bad things about the guy."

An eye roll greeted me. "It's fine. We're both moving on with our lives."

"And where are you moving on to?"

She cleared her throat and swatted away my obvious flirty tone. "So, you want to talk about Kyle yet?"

The flirt has been tucked back inside the closet. "Oh... I mean."

"Why did his dad punch you?"

I looked down at the amber-colored ale hiding behind a glass dam. I cleared my throat and clicked my tongue. "It was about the podcast."

"The Adam Benny thing?"

"No, the new one."

She sat back, confused by the news. A reaction I have come to get used to in this town.

"I know. It's a long story."

She checked the time and smiled. "It's not like this place closes anytime soon."

"Don't you have to get home to the kids or something?"

"Nick has them. I am... as free as a bird. *All night.*"

The change in her tone intrigued me. *Was Megan still interested after all of this time? Was she... flirting back?* I shook the idea out of my head and stared back at her. She asked about the new podcast, and I wasn't about to lie to her face. Or not tell her about it because she used a flirty voice.

"Right. Okay. Well, I came home when I heard about Kyle. And where Kyle did it."

Megan stared back confused. "What do you mean where he did it?"

"The suicide."

Megan's face went pale as she sat back against the booth. "Wasn't it at his house?"

I looked at her, face still white from the subject matter. I noticed the "*See Ya Soon*" neon light was back on. And the Watcher was back under it. His eyes watching my every move. I focused back on Megan.

"Umm. I probably shouldn't say anything. It's not my place."

Even though it was... *my place.*

She moved her hand across the table and put it on top of mine.

"Guess I'll just go listen to the podcast... but I'd much rather hear it from you in person."

I let out a deep sigh. *Damn it.*

"Kyle killed himself out at my old house."

She pulled her hand back and covered her shocked mouth with it.

"Oh my god!"

"Yep. It's pretty... messed up."

I glanced back at the Watcher. I still couldn't make out who it was... but he knew I knew he was watching. He delivered a slight, uncomfortable wave in my direction.

"...Paul?"

I looked back at the confused face of Megan. She turned to see what, *or who*, I was looking at.

"Did you hear me?"

I shook my head. "Sorry, what was that?"

"So then... what exactly is the new podcast about?"

Another deep-as-hell sigh rose out of the puddle of nerves in my stomach.

"It's about 8114. And trying to figure out what happened to Kyle... and why he did what he did there."

"That's... sort of sweet?"

Her response caught me off guard—

"You might be the only person that thinks that."

"He was your friend, not theirs. I think it's nice."

Would she also think it was nice if I told her that Kyle's rotting corpse was following me around and talking to me on a daily basis?

"So... are you talking to people about it?"

"Like a therapist?"

She let out a small laugh. "No, like on the podcast. Are you interviewing people or is it just you going all *Unsolved Mysteries* with it?"

"I've talked to a few people. Matt was on there," I said, wanting to follow it up with *at least I think it was Matt*, but I didn't. "I'm talking to Nancy from the Historical Museum tomorrow. I asked Chief Allan, but he said no. I'm trying to get people who spent time out there."

"At your old house?"

I gave her a nod and took a sip of my beer. *Yes.*

"I spent a LOT of time out there. Have me on it."

"Umm, are you serious?"

"I spent a lot of time out there."

"Yeah, but... you never like, saw anything. Or experienced *anything*."

She sat back and grinned. "It's about the house and Kyle, right?"

"It's a bit more complicated than that."

She shook her head and took a drink. "Listen, it's up to you. You said nobody wants to do it. I said I'll do it."

I gave a nod, letting her know she was right. Even if she didn't know what the podcast was actually about, it would still be nice to get a purely human point of Kyle and the house.

"Okay, sure. Let's schedule it in the next few days."

Her loud laugh spilled out—

"Schedule it? You're so dang professional. It's cute but... do you know how chaotic my life is right now, Paul?"

"...I don't."

"It's absolute chaos. I spend most of my time waiting for the girls to get done hanging out or doing sports or whatever it is they do," she said, taking a drink, then setting it back down. "So, I'm available tonight and tonight only. If you want me to be on your podcast, that's your only option."

That was the feeling of a nervous gulp taking a *Fantastic Voyage* all the way down my throat. "Well, I don't have any of my gear here."

Another small Megan laugh—

"Your gear? You're so fancy." She eyed me from the rim of her glass. "Where is it?"

"At my Airbnb."

"And... that is where?"

"Across from the coffee shop."

A grin formed in the corner of her mouth.

"Would you look at that. We can walk there from here."

I once again felt like a nervous high school kid holding the hand of Megan Carey. *This* was the first good, normal thing I had experienced in days, so I was expecting some horrific encounter to shatter the moment. Aside from my personal Watcher in the corner, everything had been normal. And every part of me hoped it would stay like that. I smiled back—

"I'll settle up."

Chapter Thirteen

Megan strolled around the Airbnb like she had never seen one before.

Every once in a while, she would pick up a tacky decoration on display and wave it at me. This time, it was a wooden "Live, Laugh, Love. Repeat." sign. She stared down at it in disgust.

"I hate these things."

"You hate to live, laugh, and love?"

"No. I hate signs telling me what to do."

"Like... stop signs?"

She set the wooden sign back down and flipped me off. "You know what I mean. These life advice signs that people put all over their house as a reminder to be a human or something."

Or something.

I thought about what one of those signs would say about me right now. What sort of life advice would I get from a small, cheap block of wood?

Be a piece of shit. Repeat.

Or...

You're pathetic.

Or...

You deserve all of this.

Or...

The last one awai—

That last thought sent a shiver down my spine as I continued to set-up my equipment in my makeshift dining room podcast studio. Megan finished her Airbnb investigation and plopped down. She touched the microphone sitting in front of her, causing a louder than anticipated thumping, startling both of us.

"Sorry!"

I let out a small laugh, shaking my head at her technical curiosity. "No, glad you did that. Now I know to turn your mic down." She delivered a flirty tilt of the head and grinned.

"You were always good at this stuff."

"I don't know about that."

"You were always *good*." She cleared her throat. "What happened?"

I stopped fiddling with the equalizer on my small mixer and looked across the table at her. Gone was the flirtatious smile. A concerned, somewhat disappointed lip chew had taken over her face like she'd been replaced by a body snatcher.

I thought about lying and telling her that I'm still the good person she thinks I am. The good person I always was. But the truth is, she is right. And she might be the only person in the world who isn't full-on judging me for that at the current moment. Or at least I'd like to think so. I cleared my throat to spew out my response, but she cut me off—

"That came out wrong. I'm not saying you're a bad person or anything, Paul. And I'm still going to sleep with you tonight... but—" She put her hands on her face like a worried friend and her eyes grew sad. "I just want to know what happened to you. Or... what *is* happening to you."

I stared back, enamored with the beauty that never left her. She always had a natural beauty to her. The years show in most people our age, and I saw plenty of that at Kyle's service earlier. The faces of alcoholics, lonely wives, stressed-out husbands, addicts, parents filled with regret, and depressed, old friends. Life is only friendly to those that are friendly back. That's why I look the way I do... and Megan is still an absolute treasure.

I unleashed a nervous laugh—

"I'm sorry. Did you say you were going to sleep with me?"

She rolled her eyes. "Okay. So that's all you heard, huh?"

"You know that whole in one ear, out the other thing? That statement went somewhere else."

"PAUL." A tiny, embarrassed laugh followed, and we shared a flirty, understanding grin. I sighed and bit the bullet—

"I see Kyle."

Megan looked up at me, confused by the statement.

"Like, in your dreams?"

I shook my head. "No, like, I see him. He's following me... or guiding me. Or... shit. I guess *haunting me.*"

Megan looked around the room. "Is he here now?"

I glanced up, wondering the same thing. I wasn't sure how it all worked or what the rules were. Was it like *A Christmas Carol* and Kyle only showed up to guide me through decisions or prove a point? Or was he just a bored ghost fucking with his friend because there was literally nothing else for him to do?

"I don't know."

A small shiver escaped out of Megan's back. "That's creepy."

I peered into the dark hallway just behind Megan. The outline of a body was visible, but I couldn't quite make out who it could be. Or who it was supposed to be. Or if it was actually getting closer or if my mind was playing tricks on me. I quickly put my focus back on Megan.

"Sometimes, sure. Other times, it's... nice to see him. Even though—" I let the thought trail off, leaving her hanging at the other side of the table.

"Even though what?"

"...it's the dead version of him."

She covered her mouth. "Like in that one movie... *Pet Graveyard* or something?"

"*Sematary*. And yeah, I guess it's sort of like that but even worse."

"Worse?"

"He's not the only one I see. Or... the only one haunting me." I looked down at my arm and the healing tree wound. It was suddenly open again, but instead of blood coming out of it, black, stringy hair was suddenly seeping out. I carefully pulled at it, clumping the hair in my palm. The more I held, the more came out... as if it was attached to a head. It didn't help that the yanking was making the wound even bigger. What was originally a small opening from the end of a jagged branch had now stretched into the size of a coffee cup.

The black hair was overflowing out of my wound and wrapped all around my hand. I tugged at it a few more times only to feel that it was attached to something inside my arm. I gave it one big yank and stared down into the wound, to see the eye of The Blackened Lady staring back at me.

The hair was attached to her head... *inside my skin.*

Then, her hair took on a life of its own and spread out, latching on to anything it could touch. It tightened itself around the bases of the table and chairs. A hideous, deathly growl escaped from inside the wound as The Blackened Lady began to *crawl* out of my arm. A full, rotted human pulling herself out of the innards of my limb like Samara crawling out of the well. The pain was unbearable... but so was the fact that she had her smiling face focused only on Megan.

My arm skin turned into putty as The Blackened Lady pulled her entire body out of my appendage. I screamed out loud and clamped down on my mangled, ruptured arm. The pain was—

"Paul?!"

I looked over to see Megan staring at me from the other

side of the bed. She held the blanket up to her shoulders, terrified as can be. It took me a minute to realize it was much later
in our night. We must have passed out... which led to a
terrible nightmare about—

"You're bleeding."

Megan was pointing down to my arm, where a puddle of
red had formed on the all-white sheet. I peeled the cover back
and winced in pain. The wound had reopened and was throbbing more than ever. The worst part wasn't even the pain or
Megan's terrified face.

It was the clump of charred black hair stuck to the blood-
stained sheet.

Chapter Fourteen

HTAED
HTAED
HTAED
HTAED
HTAED
HTAED
HTAED
HTAED
HTAED
HTAED
HTAED
HTAED
HTAED

I finally pulled myself out of bed late the next morning. Megan was long gone at that point. She had to pick her daughters up from Nick long before I even started stirring. I was groggy as shit. It didn't feel like a hangover. It felt like... something else. Like a heavy weight was just collapsing on me repeatedly. The throbbing in my arm pulled my attention away from my early morning blank wall stare.

There was a fresh bandage wrapped around the wound. Megan must have wrapped it after I passed out... for the second time. I thought long and hard about the night before, but I was having a hard time remembering everything that happened after we recorded her interview. I remember shots, or at least, I remember us talking about shots.

Judging by how I felt, I'd say we had plenty. *I should probably text her.*

I grabbed my phone off the bedside table and found two more emails from Producer Rachel waiting for me. I swiped them from the screen and went to my text messages. Much to my surprise, I already had a text waiting for me from Megan.

"Thanks for last night. It was good to see you... and to catch up. Hopefully my annoying voice doesn't ruin your podcast. Call me later if you want."

I smiled down at the text and typed a quick response.

"It was a GREAT night. It was nice to focus on something else for a change. And... I love your voice. It will only bring production value!"

I capped it off with one of those upside-down smiley face emojis. A moment of panic swept over me as I remembered seeing something about how that emoji is meant to be used in a sarcastic response. What if Megan read the same thing and now thinks I'm back on my bullshit with her? Or what if she prefers her smiling emojis to be right-side-up. Like a Christian and their precious wall cross. It's all hell if that thing goes upside down.

I wonder if it's the same for that damn emoji.

I considered sending a regular smiley face text to her, but three dots appeared. She was already responding so I decided to just let the antichrist smile play out. I stumbled into the kitchen and grabbed one of the coffee pods the host of the Airbnb had so graciously left. I popped it into the Keurig and grabbed an empty cup from the cupboard. The mug design made me roll my eyes—

I'll Live, Laugh, Love AFTER I Have My Coffee.

I decided to snap a picture and text it over to Megan. The three impending dots were still there, staring back at me. I held off on sending the picture in case she was on the verge of sending something serious. Nobody wants to be the guy who responds to an important text message with an ironic picture of a coffee mug.

Not even Paul Early.

I grabbed the cup and hunkered down at the kitchen table slash makeshift podcast studio. I had a few hours to kill before I had to pack all of it up and go record with Nancy at her house, so I decided to listen to the raw file of Megan's 8114 interview. I glanced down at my phone to see the three dots were still bubbling up to the surface.

Whatever it was, it could wait. I swipe locked the screen and set the phone down. I took a sip of much needed coffee and put my headphones on. I was having a hard time remembering what was said during the interview, so I was excited to dive in. A small part of me was worried about having a total *Blair Witch 2: Book of Shadows* type thing happen, and I'd stumble on some sort of horrific thing hidden in the file.

I'm not trying to be the next Jeffrey Donovan here.

I just wanted to hear what Megan had to say about Kyle, and well, everything. I grabbed my notepad and clicked play, then sipped on my coffee as the interview started—

Paul: *Alright... so... I'll introduce you and then we'll just start from there. You good?*

Megan: *Yep.*

Paul: *You sure you still want to do this?*

Megan: *Of course.*

Paul: *Okay. Then I'm ready when you are.*

Megan: *So ready. Wait. Is my voice fine? Should I use like a fake podcast voice? Something that makes me sound super important or like mysterious.*

Paul: *Just talk normal.*

Megan (using weird voice): *Like this?*

Paul: *How old are you again?*

Megan: *Wow. That's not a nice thing to ask a lady, Paul.*

Paul: *I'm introducing you now.*

Megan: *You're no fun—*

(A long sigh from Paul)

Paul: *Welcome back to 8 1 1 4, this is once again Paul Early. We're going to do things a little different on this episode. I have a very good friend here with me today to talk about Kyle and 8 1 1 4... and probably even me I would imagine. So... let's get into it. Welcome to 8 1 1 4, Megan Carey.*

Megan: *Hey Paul. Thanks for having me on.*

Paul: *Of course.*

Megan: *I've always wanted to say that.*

Paul: *Hey Paul?*

Megan: *Thanks for having me on. I feel legit now.*

Paul: *I try to make dreams come true—*

Megan: *Really? I know a few people that would say otherwise.*

(A laugh from Megan)

Paul: *Moving on... so can you tell us a bit about the relationship you had with Kyle?*

Megan: *Well, it was mostly because you and I were... a couple. That was your best friend, so he became one of my good friends. And it stayed that way even after you left—*

An unnatural fuzz took over the recording, eliminating my and Megan's voice. I rewound the recording and listened again—

Megan: *Well, it was because you and I were... a couple. That was your best friend, so he became one of my good friends. And it stayed that way even after you left—*

The same thing happened, so I hit fast forward only to be met with more fuzz and the distorted voice of my ex-girlfriend. Silence took over as I looked down to see my new bandage was now a mix of fresh blood and a spreading black growth. It wasn't like the black mold that had been haunting me. It looked as if it was... strands of hair.

A small, haunting laugh seeped into my headphones. My first thought was the recording was clearing up and maybe that was Megan laughing at my sly charm. That was quickly replaced by the realization that it was something, *or someone*, far more sinister than an ex-girlfriend.

"*Paulllllll...*"

I turned and looked down at my makeshift studio. The recording levels exploded off the charts—

"*Paulllllllllllllllll...*"

I cleared my throat, my arm and body throbbing in fear. "Hello?"

"*Thank you, Paulllll...*"

"Who... is this?"

The otherworldly fuzz once again took over.

"Who is THIS?"

The haunting chuckle returned, and goosebumps covered every inch of my skin.

"*She has such beautiful babies, Paul. Thank youuuuu...*"

My stomach dropped to the floor of the apartment. It was her... **The Blackened Lady**. And she now had her sights set on Megan and her family.

"Leave her alone."

"*Paulllllll...*"

"Please."

"*But... they could be mine... and you and her could be together forever. Don't you want that?*"

My eyes watered as I rocked back and forth in the creaking Ikea chair. It's very clear the Scandinavian chair didn't consider comfort during hauntings as a top design priority.

"*Do you????*"

My heart thumped at a rate that seemed to tell me it wanted to jump right out of my chest and *get the fuck out of dodge*. I didn't blame it one bit. Did I want to be with Megan forever? Not if it meant her losing her family. Not if it meant her walking around like Kyle's dead body. Not if it meant her getting hurt.

I've done plenty of that myself.

"No! I don't want that!" I screamed into the device. "I want you to leave me the hell alone. Leave all of us the HELL alone!" The apartment fell into silence as I wiped the frantic tears away from my face.

Did my pleading work?

Was it really that eas—

A low, haunting groan spilled out of the recording. At first it reminded me of the sound Kayako makes as she crawls down the stairs in *The Grudge*. But then I realized what it *actually* was. I forget if it was a documentary or a random internet video, but I once accidentally watched a person get hanged on camera. And while I forget exactly what the video was or where it came from, I'll never forget the sounds that man made as he hung helplessly, his legs kicking for a breath they would never get. I'll never forget that sound because it was currently escaping out of the recording.

I threw my headphones off and tried to catch my breath. I clutched my chest, trying to keep what felt like a heart attack at bay. That's when I heard the ceiling creak. I slowly lifted my head to see what it could be—

The hanging body of The Blackened Lady hung over the top of me, swaying back and forth. She smiled her black smile at me and rocked her head side to side. She was not in pain or begging for any breath she could find. No, she was enjoying *this*. She was loving *this*. I was frozen in fear as she opened her death-stained mouth.

"*Help me smile, Paul. I want her babies. Give them to meeeee.*"

I closed my eyes as tight as I could and clenched my fists. "No!!" She gave a devilish laugh at my response—

"*They could have been your babies. But... you are no good. You're like the rest of **us**.*"

I stared up at her swaying body. "That's not true! I am a good person. I am nothing like any of you." She grinned down at me.

"*You're just like us, Paul. And you'll be with **all of us** soon.*"

A collective of haunting groans and taunts suddenly filled every space in the *Live, Laugh, Love* headquarters. The place was filled with ghoulish bodies, like I was hosting a support group for the victims of 8114.

The Blackened Lady served as the Guest of Honor. Dead members of The Women of the Light worshipped her a few steps away from my shitty podcast studio.

There was a small boy, dressed as if he was a cast member of the original *Children of the Corn*. He was missing his eyes... but he was still able to stare directly at me.

A young man stared up at me from under the desk. It was hard to tell how old he was because his face and body were both heavily bloated, as if he had drowned. He puffed his lips like a fish gasping for air.

Another adult male stared at me from the shadows of the hallway. His body swayed in and out of the darkness. The only feature I could make out was his smiling face and bleeding wrists. It felt like he was hiding... or trying to figure out exactly where he was.

I knew *that* feeling all too well.

There were other haunted women, an old man in a police

uniform, young men that looked like Greasers, Native Americans, babies, people missing large parts of their bodies, a
rather demonic looking figure watching from another room,
and of course, Kyle. They all stared at me and started
breathing heavy in unison, like a mass hysteria panic attack. It
was fucking terrifying, and I desperately wanted it all to stop
before anything else happe—

Suddenly, the Airbnb ghouls all started to chant
together.

*Bye for now. And just remember, friend... don't
forget to clear your head. To give your life and join
the dead. To close your eyes and join the black.
The things out there, we want you back.*

*Bye for now. And just remember, friend... don't
forget to clear your head. To give your life and join
the dead. To close your eyes and join the black.
The things out there, we want you back.*

*Bye for now. And just remember, friend... don't
forget to clear your head. To give your life and join
the dead. To close your eyes and join the black.
The things out there, we want you back.*

Then, one by one, they all disappeared, leaving me scared
and in shock. I stared down at my podcast equipment and
screamed out. I stood up and threw it all on the ground. I was
done with all of this. It was time for me to stop giving energy
and life to that place. *To those things.* It was time for me to get
the fuck out of this town for good.

It was time for me to—

"*Paul...*"

I looked up to see The Blackened Lady was still swaying
above me.

"*We're waiting for the last one, Paul...*"

I growled at her and shook my head in frustration. "What
the fuck does that even mean?!" But before she could answer,
the rope snapped and her entire blackened, rotted body fell
on top of me, knocking us both to the ground. She grinned and

pulled herself on top of me, grinding her dead, cold body on me.

"*I want your babies, Paul...*"

I squirmed under her, trying to free myself... but she kept grinding and moaning a dead, haunted moan.

"*Why didn't you let me keep it, Paul? Whyyyy?*"

Finally, I pulled my arms from underneath her and shoved The Blackened Lady to the ground.

"**Leave me the fuck alone!!**"

I closed my eyes in a bid to hide away and—

"Paul?! What the hell!?"

I looked over to see Megan pulling herself up from the floor. She stared back in anger, pain, and confusion. I'd say mostly anger though. I sat up and realized we were both naked... and my makeshift studio was fully intact.

"I'm sorry I said that but JESUS! What the hell is wrong with you?!"

"I don't know what just happened. I'm so sorry." I said to the traumatized love of my life collecting herself on the floor.

"Fuck you, Paul. You need to figure your shit out... but it won't be with me."

"Megan, please. Let me... explain."

I watched as she pulled her clothes on, fighting off the bevy of tears trying to get out. "You told me I was the love of your life a few hours ago... but that's clearly not true."

"It *is* true, Megan. I can try to explain."

"YOU are the love of your life, Paul. It's only about YOU. That's all it will ever be."

"That's... not true."

"Really? The Adam situation. Our relationship. Hell, every relationship and friendship you've ever had. You couldn't even let Kyle rest in peace. You immediately made his fucking heartbreaking death about YOU and your stupid fucking house, Paul. And then stupid me, I open my arms back up to you. Open the idea of maybe us having that life we always talked about... the one **you** threw away. And you just... fucking toss me aside. You're no good, Paul Early. You never have been... and you never will be."

I watched as she grabbed her purse and keys, then stormed out of the apartment for good. I stood naked, looking around the quiet, empty space. Podcast equipment still on the table and no ghouls of 8114, unless of course you count me. This place was normal... and I was losing my mind. Or my grip on what was real.

Fucking Jeffrey Donovan shit.

Chapter Sixteen

I've had a ton of *woe is me* type mornings after a long night of drinking.

Mornings where I wake up with swollen knuckles or black eyes. Angry text messages. Hurt text messages. Lost belongings. Curb top parking. Explosive meetings with the porcelain god. I've had my fair share of *what the fuck happened last night*. And my fair share of *The Hulk came out again, didn't he* moments. Enough of them where I should probably consider going sober before I kill someone or kill myself.

But the feeling I had right now was something else entirely.

I wasn't in a drunken rage with Megan last night. I was being taunted by the paranormal peanut gallery. I was being fucked with by the spirits of 8114. And they really nailed the bit. I couldn't stop thinking about all the haunted faces that were staring and chanting at me inside of that apartment. I thought The Blackened Lady was the worst of them these last few days but I'm not so sure that's the case after meeting some of the others from the property. IF I actually met them. IF they were *really* there.

They.

I feel like I should have a bingo card or something to keep track of all the different ghouls and spirits... and bloated corpses. "Oh, there's the kid without eyes! Oh, OH! There's the legless old woman crying black mold! **BINGO, BABY!**"

I kept thinking about the man in the shadows that I couldn't really see and how scared he must have been. Almost like it was his first appearance at one of these group hauntings. I thought about how scared he must have been to be a new member of the 8 1 1 4 Ghoul Gang.

The 8 1 1 4 Ghoul Gang.

Jesus.

That thought immediately shifted my focus on some of the other ghouls, but mostly the demonic thing from the other room. Was that the Circle of Light fucker that everyone kept talking about?? Not to be cliché and cringe as hell, but it was like something out of a horror movie. Not like, *The Exorcist* or *The Amityville Horror* or anything like that. I'm talking about one of those new slow-burn horror movies that build something up and show this crazy fucking thing at the end. That's what *that* guy looked like. An A-Twenty-Horror show.

It felt sort of like the boss you would have to fight at the end of the video game to win the whole thing. Was that... fucking nightmare thing **The Last One** that everyone kept referring to? Because if that guy IS the last one waiting, well, he could keep on waiting for me because, and I mean this as honest as can be, absolutely **FUCK. THAT. SHIT.**

I needed to find out as much as I could about all the visitors I saw. Luckily, Nancy Hart would most likely have that 8 1 1 4 bingo card I so desperately wanted. Or at least I was hoping she would. I had no idea how the recording was going to go with her. She sent an email late last night saying she was now having second thoughts about talking. About being on the show. She had been warned and was told it would be a bad idea for *everyone* involved. I wonder who sent the warning.

Chief Allan?

The Cult of Donnie?

The Last One?

Some internet troll from the Benny Base?

I was annoyed by the momentary interference. Nancy Hart was supposed to be my golden goose. The interview that would reveal everything about this town and that house. *That fucking house.* I thought more about what she had told me about the number fourteen and Osiris. I decided I wanted to see for myself. A quick internet search brought up a bunch of different links. I clicked on the first one, which was something esoteric about Christianity and how the number fourteen means to find balance, you must suffer. Which is ironic... when you think about how Jesus was killed. Balancing on a cross while suffering his ass off.

I backed out and clicked on a link a few spots down. It described what the number fourteen represents in Tarot. The card of the Temperance. Yet another thing suggesting balance. In this case, patience, and moderation before diving into the deep end. Judging by my Airbnb filled with ghosts and demonic spirits, I'd say I left the shallow end a long fucking time ago.

I'd say I left a lot of things a long time ago.

I thought about my mom... and my friends. And everyone else in my life. I'm sure they all held or hold that *talent* against me. The fact that I can drop everything and move on. Be it belongings, places, or people. Sometimes I think I should hang a sign from my neck that says, "abandon all hope, ye who enter", just so people know what they are getting into with me. Other times, I consider it a gift. I'm sure there's a Buddha-like quote out there about how attachments are a weakness. But if this current mindfuck situation I have found myself in proves anything, it's that attachments are dangerous.

Collateral damage for the soul.

Permanent damage for the mind.

I can't help but think about where all the people in my life would be if it wasn't for me and that fucking house. Would Kyle still be alive if we were never friends? Would Matt just be focused on soccer games and baseball tournaments and gymnastics? Would Megan still be married and happy? Would my mom still be alive?

Would I be able to climb to the rafters and hang myself like Mary did?

I ignored the random, intrusive thought about dying out in that barn. That was not going to be my fate, even if Dead Kyle and the 8 1 1 4 Ghoul Gang wanted me to think so. Even if they wanted me to think that my entire life was building up to this shit show. Like it was a culmination of Adam Benny, this town, 8 1 1 4, and me. Like we are all going to collide into some bloody conclusion. **Everything has led to this!**

Bullshit.

That was not going to be the end of my story.

That was not going to be the end of *this* story.

There are people out there who believe in fate and ideas like everything happens for a reason. All the pain and hurt in this world is all for a reason. *God's plan.* Or it's to get people where they need to go. Universal signs and sways that will guide you where you need to be. Even if the *everything that happened* to you is a dead baby or a surprise suicidal best friend. That's a pretty shit way for the higher power to get you where you need to be going, right? It's THE higher power. You would think there would be an easier way to do all the things it needs to do.

For instance, if fate or *whatever it is*, wanted me to come back to 8 1 1 4, did it really need to kill Kyle? Did it really need to send a paranormal goon squad after me daily to get me there? Did it really need to do all the things it's doing that say, "Go home"? It seems like it could have taken a far less bloody and gruesome route like a twenty-year high school reunion or making me the guest of honor at one of the many parades or seasonal events this town holds.

In my opinion, a controversial podcast host would be the

perfect candidate to sit in one of those dunk tanks at the June Jamboree. The thought alone made me laugh. *Was I even controversial?* I mean, sure, I messed up, but was it a mistake worth all the scrutiny, judgment, and harassment? People fuck up. They make mistakes. That's what makes us human.

But you're not really human, Paul. You're a parasite.

I did my best to shake the voice out of the back of my head, but it stayed intact like a thought tumor, growing and overtaking every notion I had. It wasn't the first time that belief had crept into my mind. Or, into the world itself. After Adam Benny, numerous comments on social media referred to me as a "bloodsucking parasite", a tragedy leech hellbent on exploiting every drop of Benny's pain. Kyle's father accused me of doing the same thing now with his son and the 8114 podcast.

But since when is attempting to shine a light on bad things, or *evil* things, a parasitic move? Is it not philanthropical to try and shed a light on potential wrongdoings? How is what I did with the Adam Benny podcast, or what I'm currently doing with 8114, any different than one of the many true crime podcasts Netflix has adapted into award-winning miniseries? The story doesn't always stay the same, and some details come out long after the case, or podcast/series, are considered over. Stories and facts evolve over time. Sometimes those facts reveal something insidious at hand. Other times, it is all revealed to be a sham. Or the narrator had the wrong information. Or they were just simply unreliable.

It happens.

I had the wrong information about Adam Benny.

I'm working on getting the right information about 8114.

A parasite doesn't learn, it continues to do what it was meant to do: be a pest. That is not who Paul Early is. I'm misunderstood and stubborn as hell. But living off the backs of others? Profiting off their suffering and tragedy? Lying just to get a few steps ahead of everyone else?

No, that's not who I am.

I am a good person.

I will do good.

I will make everything better.

I will show everyone that my intentions were always for the best.

Sure, you will, Paul.

The ringing of my phone pulled me out of my own head. I let out a sigh, weary of what this early morning call could be. I glanced down at the screen to see it was Producer Rachel. Another sigh as I once again stepped off into the deep end—

"Hello?"

An annoyed laugh exited the other end of the phone. "Really? *Hello?* Just like that?"

A nervous wad of saliva filled my throat and my eyes darted from side to side, trying to find the perfect response. I had been ignoring Producer Rachel's emails ever since I came back home. More specifically, ever since I launched the 8114 podcast.

"I know what you're going to say, Rachel."

"I don't think that's exactly true," she cleared her throat. "You have been ignoring my emails."

"I knew you were going to say that."

"Fuck you, Paul."

I let out a deep sigh—

"I've been busy... dealing with Kyle's death."

She let out another annoyed laugh, this one overflowing with a *you can't be serious* tone.

"More like you've been busy with another exploitative podcast."

"That's not... what it is."

"Really? It's not? Because you're already lying to listeners again, Paul."

Another nervous gulp as I waited for Rachel's shoe to drop.

"That's not true. I am being one hundred percent honest and real with this—"

"Just stop, Paul. This is Adam Benny all over again... except instead of roping him and his mom into your bullshit, you're now hitching me to your full of shit pity party. I'm not going to let that happen."

"I really don't know what you're talking abou—"

"8114 is a Fleas on Parade Production, Produced by Rachel McLeod."

"Wait. Hear me out."

She laughed again, this one heavy in warning.

"No, Paul. You hear me out. Stop telling people that I'm still your producer when you know damn well that I stopped working with you after Adam Benny came forward... **the first time.** If you continue to use my name in any association with you or any one of your many bullshit, self-serving podcasts, I will sue the ever living shit out of you," She continued. "My lawyers and I will make sure you have nothing left. And I do mean NOTHING, Paul. To the point where you will have no choice but to go back to your shitty old house and rot there *forever*. You are NOT going to drag me down with you. Are we clear?"

Before I could answer, ~~Producer~~ Rachel hung up, which told me she really didn't need to hear me say *clear* back. The other shoe had dropped on Paul Early, parasite podcaster. I stared down at my phone, catching a slight reflection of myself in the broken screen. The image said so much more than words could ever say. But... words were what I needed to hear, so I spoke them to my shattered self:

I am a good person.
I will do good.
I will make everything better.
I will show everyone that my intentions were always for the best.

Then, my broken reflection replied:

Sure, you will, Paul.

PART THREE
PAUL

N ancy Hart stared back at me with her weary, judgmental eyes. She was crafting a million questions but only managed to ask one—

"How have you been sleeping, Paul?"

I let out a small *you-can-obviously-tell* laugh in response.

"I've had better nights."

"And days?" She asked, organizing the coffee table in front of us. She moved stacks of magazines and books. She set out floral coasters and placed two coffee cups down, then looked up at me, aware I hadn't answered her yet. "Paul?"

I cleared my throat, and my instincts told me to pick up the freshly placed cup to wash down whatever wouldn't clear out. It was completely empty. I glanced over at Nancy, who eyed the unfilled mug.

"I just put the pot on. I can grab you some water... or something *stronger* if you want?"

Something stronger.

That sounded nice right about now.

"It's okay, I'll wait for the tea," I said, leaving more on my tongue. "But, just out of curiosity, what does Nancy Hart consider *stronger*?"

A small grin crept out across her face.

"I'm a bourbon woman. But I'm not a picky person, Paul. I enjoy my drinks when I can. How about you?"

A small laugh fell out. I don't enjoy my drinks *when I can*. I simply enjoy them *as much* as I can. And like Nancy Hart, I'm not a picky person. Bourbon. Beer. Wine. Gin. The occasional Fireball shot. Whatever gets the job done.

"I'm not picky. But I do like my bourbon."

"I imagine before today is all said and done, we'll be having some together."

The comment made me uneasy, and she could tell. I shifted in my seat, realizing I was still holding the empty cup. I set it down and tried my best to relax. She watched my every move.

"I hope you don't mind me saying this, but you seem... off-kilter, Paul."

I scratched my chin and let my fingers move up to the side of my scruffy cheek.

"It's been an interesting few days."

She sat down across from me and put her hands under her mouth, like a therapist waiting for me to open up.

"In what ways?"

"The things I'm seeing. And experiencing," I cleared my throat. "I'm having a hard time making sense of things. I... don't know what's real anymore."

Nancy sat back, watching me through thinly opened eyes.

"What makes you think it's not *all* real, Paul?"

Her response startled me in a way I wasn't expecting. Here I was trying to make sense of everything that has happened to me since returning to this town and justify that I was possibly losing my mind. And yet, here's Nancy suggesting that it's all really happening. That everything I'm experiencing is as real as day. I blurted out an impromptu rebuttal—

"What makes *you* think it *is*?"

We could hear the teapot starting to ring out its unnerving slow whistle from inside the house. It was providing the perfect eerie soundtrack for our current discussion.

"I told you a few days ago that you should take everything serious. I meant *everything*."

"Even the gaggle of ghosts that showed up in my Airbnb uninvited?"

The teapot grew louder.

"Uninvited? Paul, you invited them into your life a long time ago by living in that house. And now you're spreading their darkness. Helping them grow. Giving them and that property a life they have never had. You're essentially holding the door open for all the evil of that place to be with you at all times."

I scoffed at her comment. "I didn't choose to live there."

The teapot reached its fever pitch as she stood up.

"True. But you did choose to go back. And that's exactly what they wanted."

She let out a sigh and stared out into our surroundings.

"I'll grab the tea. I hope this room is good for recording?"

I looked up at her—

"So, you decided to stick with the plan?"

She let out a deep sigh and nodded. "Everything has already been set in motion, Paul. Recording... or not record-ing, *that* decision won't change anything at this point."

I gave a nod. "Then... this room will be perfect."

She gave a defeated nod, then walked out of the space, leaving me on my own. I looked around at the sunroom, catching the sunshine seeping in. Nancy had filled this place with more family pictures and rustic decorations. She didn't have any old pictures of the town in here. As if this was the one place she was trying to keep safe from it. That wouldn't last long once we started recording.

I pulled out my gear and began to set up the makeshift studio on her coffee table. It was impossible not to have flash-backs to last night and this morning. When this same gear betrayed my sanity. I thought about texting Megan to see if she was okay. To apologize again about what had happened but I knew that would be a waste of time.

My recent apologies seemed to not be going over so well. Most things haven't been going over so well recently. I thought about Adam and ~~Producer~~ Rachel. Kyle and his parents. Kyle and his ~~family~~. I thought about Matt. I should call him after this to see if everything is okay. I haven't heard much from him and the last time I saw him, that damn Blackened Lady was with him, practically puppeteering his emotions. Maybe this interview with Nancy would help me figure out a way to save him and his family.

Figure out a way to save me.

There was an eerie, judgmental laugh in the back of my mind.

You heard Kyle. There is no saving you, pal.

I shook it off like all the other negative thoughts that had suddenly taken root inside my head. There had to be a way to change things. To make everything better. That's how these stories go. Someone finds themselves in a heap of paranormal, or evil, trouble and they seek help when they are at the end of their rope.

I'm at the end of my rope, hanging from a barn rafter.

Not yet... but soon.

I smacked my head, hoping to knock the thought away. I needed the help. I needed my own movie desperation scene.

I was Carolyn Perron, begging Lorraine Warren to help me.

I was the Freeling family, turning to Zelda Rubinstein's Tangina.

I was Renai Lambert turning to Lin Shaye's Elise Rainier.

I was desperate and I needed Nancy Hart to free my soul.

To cleanse my house.

I needed Nancy Hart to tell me everything was going to be okay.

I could see that wasn't going to be the case as she reentered the room with the tea kettle. Her mouth was twisted in shock and her eyes stared back at me, like they held a dark secret.

"I just heard some terrible news, Paul."

I let out a deep sigh. "Is it about me... or 8114?"

She gave a sad nod and poured the fresh, hot tea into our waiting cups.

"It's... about all of it."

All of it.

Well, that's what this podcast was supposed to be about. The goal was to reveal things as the series went on, no matter what they were. And no matter who, or what, they involved. I needed to remain true to that approach, regardless of what Nancy Hart's horrified eyes were telling me.

"Save it for the interview."

She looked up at me in shock, nearly spilling the boiling tea out onto the floor of the sunroom.

"You can't be serious?"

"I am. I set out to tell whatever truths were discovered. So, if something else has happened or has been uncovered, save it for our recording."

"But Paul... it's about—"

I raised my hand, cutting her off mid-sentence.

"I don't want to hear it until it's time to hear. Besides, it'll be better if you get my real reaction. That will play better for the listeners."

"You should be concerned about how it plays for *them*."

"Who?"

She let out a deep sigh—

"Your followers."

I let out a small laugh and plugged in the final cord to my equipment.

"I'm not worried about social media, Nancy."

"That's not what I'm talking about."

I glanced up at her, to see her eyes were focused behind me. Her grip on the tea kettle turned her knuckles white as

can be. I crinkled my face and turned to where she was looking. I wish I hadn't. The ghosts of 8114 were standing outside
of the sunroom, watching my every move. And Nancy could
see them.

It was all real.

And all terrifying.

8114 – Episode Two:
History Lesson
May 30th, 2025

H ey there everyone.

Thank you for tuning back in. I'm Paul Early... and this is **8114**. It's been a bit of a wait for this second episode to come together. As you can imagine, I've been juggling a lot of things since I've been back home. And as you can probably assume, some people aren't exactly pleased about my latest endeavor. One of them being my former producer, Rachel McLeod. I want to take this moment to point out that she is NOT a part of this podcast. And... she does NOT support it. Believe me. If you ever hear her talking about this podcast, something has gone seriously wrong. I wish her nothing but the best as we both move on from the Adam Benny podcast.

And move on I shall. Like I said, a lot of people aren't exactly happy about this podcast. I've been judged, yelled at, and even punched in the face because of it. But... I remain committed to this show. I'm not doing it for them, or for myself.

The whole point of this podcast is to figure out what happened to my friend Kyle. That's the number one goal. And to do that, I need to find out the things that have happened out at 8114. I'm not talking about things that happened when I *lived there, I mean things that have happened throughout the history of that property. Long before my family and I arrived.*

Long before Kyle.

Today's guest is going to help us do just that. Nancy Hart has been operating the Pendleton Historical Museum for the last forty-five years. Her job is literally the history of this town and to know everything that has happened in and around our community. I've known her most of my life and I'm eager, nervous, and scared to hear what she has to say about this place... and 8114.

Thank you so much for being on the show, Nancy.

Nancy: *Don't thank me yet, Paul.*

Paul: *Right. So... before we dive into everything else... let's start with* **you**. *You've lived here your entire life. You not only seem happy about that decision, but you also seem* **proud** *of that fact. What made you want to dedicate your life to protecting the history of this place?*

Nancy: *It just felt like my purpose. This place has always been good to me... but it hasn't always been* **good**.

Paul: *And that's exactly why you're here to talk.*

Nancy: *One of the reasons, yes. I'm also here to talk about you and that property. And...* **other** *things.*

Paul: *Let's save some of that for later. I'd like to start with the town if that's okay with you.*

Nancy: *Before we begin, I think we should probably inform your listeners that they are potentially opening themselves up to... harm by listening to this.*

Paul: *Are you implying that they could get... hurt by a podcast?*

Nancy: *Not like before. This isn't like your other show, Paul. That one caused a different kind of pain. This podcast, **8114**, is giving life to something... you don't quite understand.*

Paul: *Then why are you here?*

Nancy: *Because it's too late for us. Like I said before we started, everything has already been set in motion. Our fate has been sealed long before you hit that record button. But you already know that—*

Paul: *I don't think I believe in fate, Nancy. Not the kind you're talking about.*

Nancy: *Well, **you** should start believing in it. You should start believing in a lot of things, Paul. And you really need to start listening.*

Paul: *That's what we're here to do.*

Nancy: *But is that what YOU are here to do? Are you interested in listening and learning... or are you interested in hiding?*

Paul: *I'm here to listen to you tell me stories about this town. About that property.*

Nancy: *I'm afraid I can't do that, Paul.*

Paul: *Okay then. Maybe you can tell me this. Who warned you about coming on here to talk about everything?*

(Nancy clears throat, a rather heavy amount of phlegm in it—)

Nancy: *That's not important, Paul. What is important... is the fact that we are on limited time. You AND I...*

Paul: *I really don't understand.*

Nancy: *You will. I need you to listen to me, Paul. Do you remember Camp Chesterfield?*

Paul: *Of course. The psychic camp...*

Nancy: *Spiritual Center.*

Paul: *Right. What about it?*

Nancy: *The call I received before we started recording today was from my friend Marion. She spends time out there... and has a certain connection with the spirit world.*

Paul: *Wow. Really? Did she have a message for me from the afterlife?*

Nancy: *Paul. This is serious.*

Paul: *Okay. What did your friend Marion say?*

Nancy: *She said a lot of things... but this was more about what she heard. What exactly does this mean—**don't forget to clear your head. To give your life and join the dead. To close your eyes and join the black. The things out there, they want you back.***

(Uncomfortable shifting—)

Paul: *Where, umm, where did she hear that?*

Nancy: *During a reading out at the camp. She was terrified by whatever it was, Paul.*

Paul: *How did she know it was **for** me?*

Nancy: *We had lunch the day you came into the museum. She could feel that energy on me. Like... whatever was following you was suddenly following me. And then, it followed her. In the two days since that lunch, she's had horrible visions about what's going to happen to me. And to you.*

Paul: *What's going to happen to us?*

Nancy: *I already told you our fates were sealed, Paul.*

Paul: *I don't believe that.*

Nancy: *Failure to believe it won't stop this from happening. You just can't pull the blanket over your eyes and hope the scary thing leaves. The thing is already **inside** the blanket with you, Paul. The thing IS the blanket. It's all around you. And when this is all said and done, it's going to cover you from head to toe. Like a burial sheet.*

Paul: *I don't bel—*

Nancy: *Where have you heard that message before?*

Paul: *I've heard it over and over. Mostly since I came back home.*

Nancy: *From who?*

Paul: *The dead.*

Nancy: *The ones I saw today?*

Paul: *And more.*

Nancy: *I recognized some of them.*

Paul: *Some of the... ghosts?*

Nancy: *Yes.*

Paul: *How?*

Nancy: *They lived here. And they died—*

Paul: *Out there?*

Nancy: *Yes. And here.*

Paul. *That... can't be true.*

Nancy: *I saw them, Paul. I know those faces.*

Paul: *I don't beli—*

Nancy: ***Mary. Isabelle.*** *The other Women of the Light.*

Paul: *Isabelle? That's who Ma—*

Nancy: ***The Boy with No Eyes.*** *He was found on that land... not long after his family settled here. They accused a group of Native Americans.*

Paul: *The Fall Creek Massacre?*

Nancy: *Yes. And more.* ***The Drowned Man.*** *Alec Munson. His mother killed him and dumped him inside the* *well out there. He only wanted to get married... and she hated his fiancée. So, she poisoned him. That poison seeped into the water supply. Into the soil.* **Sheriff Raglan**. *He was investigating an armed robbery and heard the folks responsible were hiding out in those barns. He was shot five times at close point... and died in the small barn. His wife took over... and died three months later... in a car accident directly in front of the property.* **Babies. Native Americans.** *That land has seen and tasted more blood than you can imagine, Paul.*

(*Nancy clears her throat again, still heavy on the phlegm—*)

Paul: *What is the demon?*

Nancy: *The what?*

Paul: *There was this... thing. It was slouched and watching me. Smiling at me.*

Nancy: *I... don't know, Paul.*

Paul: *Would Marion?*

Nancy: *Possibly.*

Paul: *Call her.*

Nancy: *I don't know if that's a good idea. She wouldn't want to be involved in the recording.*

Paul: *You said it's already following her.*

Nancy: *Fine.*

(*A brief pause, the ringing of a phone*)

Marion (on phone): *...Nancy?*

Nancy: *Hi, Marion. I'm here with Paul Early. We're recor—*

Marion (on phone): *I don't understand. I told you what would happen if you met with him, Nancy.*

Nancy: *I know, I just—*

Paul: *Marion, I need your help with something.*

(A long pause—)

Marion (on phone): *I can't help you, Paul. I shouldn't even be on the phone with **you**.*

Paul: *I've been seeing things. Ghosts or... spirits. Or whatever you want to call them. But... I also saw this demon-looking thing. Do you know what it would be?*

Marion (on phone): *It's everything. It's that house. That land. It's life. It's your mistakes. Your past. Your present. Your future. I'm sorry to say this... but it's your reckoning, Paul.*

Paul: *How do I stop it?*

Marion (on phone): *You don't. **It wants you back...***

Paul: *No, I refuse to believe that. Kyle has to be the last one it takes—*

Marion (on phone): *Wait, you didn't tell him yet, Nancy?*

Nancy: *I tried... he wanted to wait.*

Paul: *Tell me what??*

Marion (on phone): YOU *will be the last one it takes, Paul. Your friend Kyle wasn't the last person to die there.*

Paul: *What do you mean? What's she mean, Nancy?*

Nancy: *I'm so sorry, Paul.*

Paul: *About what?*

Marion (on phone): *There's a new spirit following you. Have you seen it?*

Paul: *No...?*

Marion (on phone): *Are you sure? It would seem... confused. Almost scared—*

Paul: *There was this... one the other night. Who is it??*

(*Static interferes—*)

Marion (on phone): *Nancy... you need to leave while you still—*

(*The phone goes dead—*)

Paul: *...who was it?*

Nancy: *Matt Roberts was found inside your house this morning.*

Paul: *No... that can't be—*

Nancy: *His family... they were found in the barn.*

Paul: *No, no, no...*

(*Nancy wheezes—*)

Nancy: *You asked how you can stop it. Stop all this pain... and hurt... and madness. There is a way—*

Paul (through tears): *Tell me...*

Nancy (distorted/pained): *Let them have you back. Let that place swallow you whole. Let that place—*

Chapter Eighteen

Nancy Hart stared back at me from across the room—

The microphone sat in front of her lifeless body. The equalizer sat still as if it was afraid to move or register a sound. I felt the same way. I had known this woman my entire life... and now she was dead in front of me. And I had recorded her final moments.

I had recorded her... death.

Her last gasp of desperation.

Let that place swallow you whole.

The same place that took so many lives. That was *still* taking so many lives. I couldn't take my eyes off her body BUT I needed to see if the Matt news was real. If I had lost another friend. If another family was ripped apart. If this town was going to chase me out. I also needed to tell someone about Nancy... but my body and mind were preventing me from moving or even deciding on how to move forward.

We were just having a full-on conversation five minutes ago. She just brewed us a kettle of tea not even an hour ago. Now, she sat slumped in lifeless horror across from me. An entire lifetime in this town, ending in a desperate plea to what? *Sacrifice myself to that land?*

Fuck that.

I was intent on staying the hell away from that place forever. At this point, I was strongly considering packing all my shit and hightailing it out of this town forever. Kyle's gone. If Nancy and Marion are telling the truth... then Matt is also gone.

Jesus.

There's nothing left for me in this town. Nothing but anger and judgment. This place will surely tie me to a stake and burn me alive if that means no more suffering and pain. No more dead families. No more curses. No more 8114. **No more Paul Early.** Maybe that's what the world needs.

Maybe that's what I need.

The buzzing of Nancy's cell phone pulled me out of my personal pity party. I stared down to see Marion was calling. Fear took over every bit of my skin as I stared down at a picture of the two women hugging in front of the waterfall. I didn't know how long they had been friends or how long they had even known each other.

I just knew Nancy was dead and Marion told her it would happen.

We were both in the same pair of haunted shoes. Both wondering if our friends were alive. Or if they were burning in 8114 hell. I couldn't bring myself to answer the phone. Part of me hoped that Nancy would suddenly spring forward and answer it with a joyful tone.

The other part of me knew that wasn't going to happen.

If Nancy Hart sprung forward, it would be at the devilish whim of a cursed land. The thought alone made me wince in horror. I stared back at her, still unsure of how to proceed. I eyed my own phone and considered calling 911. Or Chief Allan. But I knew that his hands were waist-deep in Paul Early's shit storm.

I thought about calling Matt even though I knew he wouldn't pick up.

I thought about calling Megan.

I could even go for a small talk with ~~Producer~~ Rachel right about now.

But I didn't call any of them.

I just stared at the broken, black screen and shoved it back into my pocket. I looked out at Nancy and her shocked open mouth. My eyes watered for the poor woman across from me. I didn't know much about her outside of her love for the history of this town. The same history that most likely stopped her heart. I knew her husband passed away a few years ago. I knew they didn't have any children. I knew that most folks wouldn't even bat an eye at her loss. And that as far as people outside this small town were concerned, she would just be another name on a gravestone as they drove by on a road trip.

Nancy Hart deserved better than that.

She deserved better than a death by podcast. She deserved to—

Be with the things out there.

I kicked the intrusive thought out of my head and looked back at the dead woman across from me. Her gaping maw was suddenly... *closed?* How was that even possible? Was she still... alive? I pulled myself out of my chair and slowly approached Nancy, nervous as hell.

Her phone buzzed. Marion's picture once again graced the phone screen, and I considered answering it with a jubilant "She's alive!" ... but as I reached for it, I noticed Nancy's mouth slowly fall back open from the corner of my eye.

I took a step back, leery of whatever the fuck was about to happen. Suddenly, two bloated fingers felt around her dead lips from *inside* of her mouth. A painful groan fell out behind them.

"Mom?? Please... let me out of here. I won't marry her."

The moist, gray fingers kept feeling around for anything to grab onto—

"Mom. I don't feel good. It hurts. Why would you do this to me???"

I realized that I was hearing the voice of Alec Munson. The man who was put in a well just because he wanted to get married. Wanted to love someone for the rest of his life. And it got him killed. By his own mother.

I thought about my mom again. Naked and alone, running around those barns. We were the reverse. I left her alone out there to die. I just didn't know it. I rubbed my head and tried to shake the thought. But Alec's haunted voice rang out from inside Nancy again.

"Mom, pleaseeee."

Alec's dead, bloated fingers stopped dancing around her cold lips... and pointed straight at me.

"You belong with us, Paul. Drowning in your misery and destruction."

I shook my head, doing my best to keep the shivers at bay. I closed my eyes and called out to the voice inside Nancy—

"You're not real. None of this is real!"

I reopened them to see Alec Munson sitting where Nancy's body was. His wet, dead body dripped onto the floor. His lips puckered and his grotesque, gray fingers danced on the arm of the chair. He giggled at my horror.

"It will only hurt for a little bit, Paul. But you deserve so much more pain."

I stumbled backwards, falling into my chair. As I landed, Alec launched out of his chair and slimed his way across the floor at me. His bloated hands gripped onto my ankles, and he pulled his sopping body up onto my lap. His rotted face pushed into mine as he opened his saggy mouth.

"Let us swallow you whole."

I started to black out as Alec placed his moist, dead lips around my head. He moaned in wet pleasure as the voices of 8114 filled the room with their giggles. The very last thing I saw was black mold covering Nancy Hart's entire dead body.

Swallowing her whole.

Chapter Nineteen

I woke up, shivering and uncomfortable.
My back was cold from the slab of concrete under it. I quickly sat up and realized I was surrounded by concrete walls... with bars directly in front of me. My confusion was quickly overtaken by a very big **OH SHIT**.

I was in a holding cell at the police station.

I rubbed my neck and quickly thought back to the wet Alec attack that had just happened in Nancy Hart's sunroom. I wasn't sure how much time had passed since he mopped my face with his. I wasn't even sure if it was the same day. I dragged my hand across my scruffy face just in case he left some drool. There was just mine.

Hopefully.

"Nice of you to finally join us."

I looked over, expecting to see one of the 8114 ghouls talking to me. Instead, it was Deputy Ryan Simms. An ex-football star who turned his high school glory days into a harassment hall pass.

"Ryan," I said, rubbing the back of my head as I approached the bars. "You guys just letting me sleep something off... or is there more to this little charade?"

Deputy Simms sized me up from his side of freedom and shook his head.

"You've pissed a lot of people off, Paul. And now bodies are piling up all around you. I'd love to keep you in there as long as possible."

I could see that every wrinkle forming in his skin had anger for me. I figured my best plan of action was not to engage with his police rage and instead aim for what was behind the badge. The heart of a former classmate.

"Is it true about Matt?" I asked, hoping that Marion and Nancy were wrong. Ryan's face sunk and he gripped one of the bars.

"It's true. And it's fucking awful."

"What happened?"

He sighed and let the bar go. "I think it's best if I let the Chief talk to you about everything. I was just here to make sure you woke up."

"You guys don't think I'm responsible for all of this, do you?"

He sighed and rubbed his head. A brief shake later and he nodded at me. "Again, I think it's best if the Chief does the talking." With that, Deputy Simms unlocked the cell and escorted me out of my temporary home.

We walked through the station, passing shocked faces left and right. Some were officers from town, others wore state and county badges. That made sense to me since the Indiana State Police post was down the road a bit from 8114.

Multiple people were organizing paperwork and filling coffee mugs. The phones were ringing off the hook. It felt like a newsroom scene in a movie where a big break had just come in. Everything turned to slow motion as we walked by. Or maybe I just *wanted* it all to be in slow motion so I could avoid getting to our destination.

Simms knocked on the half-open door in front of us.

"Chief? Got Paul Early here." He pushed open the door and motioned for me to enter. Feeling small as hell, I entered

Chief Allan's office to see a tired, frustrated version of the Chief staring back at me. He looked... withered. Like something was eating AT him and THROUGH him. Simms gave a quick nod, then disappeared back into the chaos of the station.

I took my seat and stared back at the shell of the man in front of me. He leaned back in his chair, groaning in deep pain as he did.

"I feel like I've been sitting in this chair for a week straight," he said, eyeing me from across the desk. "How'd you sleep?"

"I don't really know."

He gave a nod then took a sip of his coffee. I rubbed my head, feeling more hungover than tired. I realized I still had no idea what day it was.

"How long was I out?"

"Just overnight. You were passed out when we found you... figured the safest thing to do was to put you into holding for the night."

"Because... you think I'm responsible?"

He took off his reading glasses and pinched the top of his nose—

"I think that... there are things at play here that involve you. Do I think that means you bear the responsibility? I'm undecided, Paul."

A sigh of relief spilled out and I sunk a little deeper into my chair.

"I'm here to help, Chief."

He gave a quick tilt of the head—

"Are you? Because I'm pissed as hell right now. You've done a lot of damage and I have no idea what's going to happen next. Or whose body I'm going to find. Or what it all means. I just know it's all coming back to **you**."

Yep. That's what I keep hearing, Chief.

I took a deep breath—

"That's what I'm trying to figure out with the pod—"

I stopped and looked up at Chief Allan, glaring back at me for even thinking about using that word in his office.

"That's done now, Paul. There is no podcast."

"What do you mean?"

He let out the kind of laugh an angry parent lets out when their misbehaving child just isn't getting it.

"What do you think I mean? There will be no more episodes or reveals or any of your bullshit. There will be nothing BECAUSE WE ARE INVESTIGATING MULTIPLE DEATHS. You already revealed sensitive information about the case that I specifically asked you not to. Your little 8114 show is over."

I stared back at him, trying to formulate a proper response in my head. I didn't have any bosses with 8114. I didn't have a producer. I didn't have sponsors. I only had myself and the story. And the story was still revealing itself. It was still being written.

It was **still** going to happen.

"You can't do that."

"Then explain to me how you're going to record without all of your fancy equipment?"

"Excuse me?"

He shook his head and threw his hands up—

"It's evidence, Paul."

"Evidence for what?! There wasn't a crime committed."

He gave a nod, then slid over a piece of paper with scribbled handwriting on it.

"Do you know a Marion Harrison?"

I sighed and sat back in the chair, playing the role of pouty child to a tee.

"I know *of* her. She is Nancy's... *was* Nancy's friend."

"She has reason to believe that you recorded the final moments of Nancy Hart's life. Is that true?"

Was it true? I hadn't had a chance to go back and listen to the interview, so I had no idea if I actually captured it. Or if it was blocked out by a paranormal fuzz. Part of me hoped I caught it... because that would make for quite the urban legend.

It would make 8114 legendary.

Me legendary.

Then again, this podcast wasn't about me. It was about Kyle. It was about that house. *Right.* That house. I looked up at Chief Allan—

"Well, in my defense, Marion Harrison also thinks that 8114 is a demonic entity out to get me."

He sat back in his chair and sized me up. "Isn't it though? And isn't that what **you** believe, Paul?"

I looked back at the Chief as my thoughts danced across the office. I could continue to play oblivious and stubborn. Or I could take the moment to have an honest interaction with a man going through the same shit—

"I don't know what I believe anymore, Chief," I said, dropping a massive exhale right after. "All these terrible things keep happening around me... or out at that house... and I don't know what to think anymore."

He leaned forward and merged his hands into a triangle under his chin.

"Have you ever heard of *Operation Fantasia?*"

I shook my head *no*, so he continued—

"After the attack on Pearl Harbor, American scientists developed several *unique* strategies to fool the Axis enemies. One of these strategies came from a psychological warfare strategist named Ed Salinger," he sat back and continued. "Salinger was an expert in Japanese culture. He knew the art, the language, the music, the food. He knew everything... including their superstitions. One of them being about magic fox-shaped spirits called **kitsune**. It was his belief that if they could somehow craft fake kitsune, it would scare the Japanese soldiers out of the fight. Or at least make them think that something supernatural was afoot. The plan started with balloons and eerie whistles. Then they wanted to paint real foxes with glow in the dark paint... that had radium. That didn't work either. They tried a few more harebrained ideas that failed to get out of testing. All in all, Operation Fantasia was a failure from the start."

I sat back in disbelief—

"Is that real?"

"100%."

"Are you trying to tell me there are radium-painted ghosts out at 8114?"

"No, Paul. I'm trying to tell you that sometimes people, *or things*, want you to see stuff a certain way to scare the fight out of you. To make you believe what they want you to believe. But sometimes that want is overshadowed by a misunderstanding of what they are truly fighting. You see, Salinger and those scientists thought that painting foxes would scare the same group that just killed over two thousand people at Pearl Harbor. You can't defeat that sort of evil with glow in the dark animals. You defeat that sort of evil by making sure they are never a threat again."

"Do you want me to drop an atomic bomb on 8114, Chief?"

He sat back and let out a deep, sorrowful sigh.

"No, Paul. I just don't want you to underestimate that place."

I thought about this for a moment. Is that what I had been doing up to this point? Underestimating 8114 and everything around it? Was I in a war with whatever it represented? And Kyle and Matt and Nancy were all just collateral damage? Maybe it did all end with me like Marion suggested. Maybe everyone else would be safe if I just went home.

I am the radioactive one at this point.

Everything I touch spreads sickness.

It causes pain and horror. I hurt whoever I cross paths with.

I am a product of a war.

One with myself.

With kindness.

With honesty.

With taking responsibility.

With not tightening the noose as tight as possible and jumping from the rafters.

I looked up at Chief Allan. His eyes had grown heavier since this talk began. We both realized we had yet to bring up the hardest part of our days—

"What happened?" I asked.

"Do you really want to know, Paul?"

I was feeling déjà vu. This was oddly similar to the conversation we had in front of the big barn after Kyle's death. And just like that, the very quick and obvious answer was once again *no*. **HELL no.** But the longer, more tangled answer—like the black, moldy hair of a ghost—was **YES**.

"Yes."

He let out a deep sigh and eyed the door. Then—

"Matt Roberts took his wife and daughters out to that damn place. He lit all three on fire and hung them from the rafters. Then, he walked into the house and slit both wrists in one of the upstairs bedrooms."

I couldn't hold it in. I vomited all over the Chief's office. Matt loved his family. He loved his daughters. He would never hurt them like that. He would never do anything like that.

But... she would.

I wiped my mouth and looked up at the watery-eyed Chief of police. "Which room?"

"What?"

"Which room did he do it in?"

He nodded—

"The one in the middle, right in front of the staircase."

Shit.

"That was my bedroom," I said, doing my best to hold in a second round of vomit. "Why do you have reason to believe he did all of that? Do you know for a fact?"

"Yes."

"How?! How the hell do you know Matt did that?!"

The Chief wiped his eyes and pulled out a small video-tape from his top drawer.

"Because we watched him do it."

I stared down at the videotape and lost another round of my stomach. Then I lost all the tears my eyes were holding back. I screamed out in pain and hurt as the Chief came around his desk. He put his hand on my shoulder as I continued to let everything out. Deputy Simms rushed into the office with some water and towels. I was a blubbering mess and I just wanted to leave. I wanted to leave forever.

Soon, Paul.

But I needed to know something else. Something that didn't make any sense. I waited until Deputy Simms left the office and waited as someone cleaned up my vomit. I reclaimed my seat and stared at the videotape. The Chief stared back—

"What are you thinking about, Paul?"

"Did you watch it until the end?" I asked, scared of what his answer would be.

"I watched more of that tape than I wanted to. It's... going to haunt a lot of people around here."

You have no idea, Chief.

"I understand... but I just need to know something."

"What's that?"

I rubbed my head and took a big, nervous gulp.

"Who was holding the camera?"

I watched as Deputy Simms pulled away from Nancy's house.

My car was still parked in front of her home, waiting for us to finish recording. It wasn't the only thing waiting. An older woman watched my every move from the darkness of Nancy Hart's porch. She sipped from a cup and rocked back and forth in an old wooden chair. I cleared my throat and clutched the leather satchel hanging by my side. I dug for my keys and made my way for the driver's side door when—

"Paul Early."

I turned back to the porch; the woman was now standing on the top step. I could see who it was now as clear as day. Marion Harrison had been waiting for me to return.

She wasn't the only one—

I once again cleared my throat and gave a gentle nod. "I'm sorry for your loss." I didn't know if Marion Harrison was looking for a confrontation or a conversation. I truly wasn't interested in either one. I was only interested in what I had waiting for me deep inside my satchel. It was the only thing I needed answers from. I unlocked the driver's side door and opened it, prepping my escape when—

"Belial."

I stopped moving and looked over to Marion, who was inching closer to my parked vehicle.

"Excuse me?"

"You asked what the demon was. You know him as the Circle of Light. But his name is Belial. And he has found a home with you, Paul." She shrunk her eyelids, as if she was trying to read my thoughts. *Or my fear.*

"I thought you said it was the house."

"I said it was *everything*. It's possible to be haunted by demons and the demons of your past at the same time."

You don't say.

"What does he want with me?" I asked, genuinely curious about my demonic stalker.

Marion shook her head and her mouth cracked open with a sinister grin. Like I was an idiot for even thinking this current situation of mine could be explained. She took a few steps closer, her steps slower and more unnatural with every touch of the pavement. She was now standing next to the passenger side window, staring at me over the hood of the car.

"Want? Nothing. He's feeding off you. Off all of **this**."

"*This?*"

She continued to grin at me—

"All the pain and hurt you have caused, Paul Early," her voice morphed into a slightly distorted version of itself. "All of the hell. All the sickness. All the DEATH."

I pulled my satchel closer to the side, as if I was protecting the contents with my life. She was making me nervous. *Uneasy.* Truthfully, she was scaring the hell out of me—

"Why?"

Her voice grew deep, like someone else was using it.

"Belial is the demon of impurity and lies. What exactly are you, Paul Early?"

I looked back at her from across the hood of the car—

"I'm *none* of those things."

She let out a loud laugh, letting her fingers drag across the roof of the rental. Scared and over this exchange, I climbed into the driver's side door and started the ignition. Marion stayed just outside of the passenger door... but she wouldn't have any problem keeping the conversation going. Much to my dismay, I had left the windows down in the car. It was a hot Indiana day yesterday... and none of *this* was supposed to happen.

I quickly put my finger on the passenger side window mechanism and started to raise it up. In a horrifying flash, Marion took hold of the rising window with both hands, hissing as I tried to raise it.

"There is no running from this, Paul. There is no hiding."

As the window slowly raised, Marion began to crunch the rising glass with her grip, splitting it into jagged shards.

"We're all waiting for **you**."

As the jagged window continued to rise, she let out a hideous laugh and smashed her neck down on the broken edges. She stared at me as she dragged her neck across the glass, cutting her skin open into a torn gash of blood and gore. I screamed out in horror as she continued to stare at me. The broken window was damn near through the back of her neck at this point.

"It's time to come home, Paul."

And with that, she pushed her body away from the passenger side of the car with a massive amount of force, pulling her head off completely! I gasped in shock as both her head and body collapsed outside of the car. I screamed out in horror and panic and glanced down at my satchel, then back at the road. I shifted the car into drive and pulled away from the horrors of Nancy Hart's house as fast as I could.

As I begged my body for air, I glanced in the rearview mirror to see Marion's headless body sitting next to The Blackened Lady and the demon I saw a few nights before: **Belial**. I didn't have any time to process the fear because something smashed through my windshield and landed with a thud in the passenger seat.

I turned and let out a horrified scream.

It was a newborn baby... still attached to a noose—

Chapter Twenty-One

I searched one of the Airbnb hallway closets in a panicked frenzy.

I remember a section in the *welcome* binder where they mentioned they had vintage electronics for guests who wanted to feel nostalgic. There were multiple storage containers each filled with devices and taped on Ziplock bags with the needed cords. So far, I had found a Gameboy, Sega Genesis, a Dreamcast, every form of Nintendo, and PlayStation one through three.

I popped the lid off another container and found what I was looking for: an old Panasonic Omnivision VCR. I pulled it out of the closet and headed for the living room TV set. Sweat had started to drip from my forehead as I hooked up the old equipment to the new flat screen. My phone buzzed in my pocket, but I completely ignored it.

I was only focused on one thing.

I buried my hand into my satchel and pulled out the videotape Chief Allan had in his office. I assumed at this point he probably already knew I stole it... and was most definitely already sending some of his officers out to find me regarding Marion's dead body.

If Marion was in fact dead.

I had no clue if *that* entire scene I witnessed was real.

If any of *this* was even real.

I had no fucking clue what was *actually* going on right now.

I only knew that I needed to watch that tape and find out who was recording it. Maybe they would have the answers I needed. Maybe they would lead me in the right direction. Or maybe they'd just be another 8114 ghoul messing with my head. There was only one way to find out.

I pushed the tape into the VCR slot and took a step back. I scratched my nervous skin and realized my small wound was spreading and pulsating down my arm. *It hurt like hell.* Everything did. I shook my head and brushed the horror out of it for the time being, focusing my eyes back on the grainy screen. Watching this was going to hurt more than any open, infected wound. The raw footage started—

It was... *me?*

Well, ten-year-old me, running around the grounds of 8114. The footage was from my birthday that year, and I suddenly realized tomorrow was my 43rd birthday. The thought didn't cross my mind until I saw the date on the video. I remember that birthday and the bug water gun I was holding vividly. That wasn't a particularly great birthday. I invited a bunch of classmates to a party and none of them came. So, it was just me and a bug-shaped water gun.

That was one of my only birthday presents that year.

Well, that and a couple hand drawn movie tickets for *Batman Returns*. It was going to open a few weeks after my birthday. So, my mom made it known it would be included with my presents that year. Whoever was behind the camera handed the oversized device off to me.

There was the awkward up-the-nostril shot made famous a few years later in *The Blair Witch Project*. Back then, it was just made weird by a ten-year-old kid trying to get a handle on the moviemaking machine. Moments later, the camera was focused on the interior of the big barn. Then, my ten-year-old voice rang out:

"You want a tour?"

I watched as 1992 me moved through the structure, narrating the walk like he was making a found-footage movie.

"This is the main floor of the big barn. A lot of stuff down here..."

The camera spun around, making me feel slightly nauseous. I watched the darkness closely, waiting for something to jump out or stalk us. Younger me kept the tour going, focusing the camera on the old, wooden staircase. The camera raised up, revealing the second floor of the barn. It was an eerie shot, one that would make any horror director proud.

"We'll hang out up there in a little bit."

I gasped as the innocent comment served as an eerie precursor to the footage of Matt and his family. I didn't have time to process it because we kept moving. I could have sworn I saw an elderly woman run by naked as young me took us through the darkened barn. I scrambled to find the remote to the VCR just in case anything else happened on this blast from the past tour.

"Now to the creepy stuff..."

I took a deep breath as we moved out of the big barn and back onto the concrete area between the big barn and the pig barn. The footage creeped me out even though nothing horrific or haunting was happening. It was just a casual walk through an area I tried my best to avoid.

Chills went down my spine as we closed in on the small wooden structure.

I sat in front of the TV like Joaquin Phoenix in *Signs*, holding my mouth in fear as the camera focused on the two doors of the pig barn. The one on the left went into an empty room that led to the small attic. The door on the right led to the pig stalls. I practically begged younger me to not take us into the right side—

"I hate this one. This is where I first saw him..."

First saw him.

I fell to my ass and tilted my head, trying to think of what he/I was talking about. We took a few steps closer to the two doorways. *Please go left, please go left—*

Young me crossed into the right side of the pig barn. Every breath I had left my body as we slowly made our way through the six stalls. They were as creepy as ever and I still hated them with every fiber of my soul. Regardless of how much sun there was, this side always stayed dark.

I wondered if we'd go full found-footage and switch to night vision.

We never did as we made our way through the room. I leaned closer, convinced I could hear running footsteps and maniacal screaming in the distance. We slowly passed stall one, stall two, stall three, and stall four. I was terrified as we got closer to stall five. Younger me slowed to a scared as hell pace and let out a whisper—

"We're almost... there."

The camera focused on stall five as the sound of rustling was heard. There was something moving in stall six. *Something waiting for us.* I wanted to scream out for *us* to run away, to get the hell out of there. But I knew that was pointless. Because I never left. I now remembered this day clearly. I remembered this exact moment.

This exact hell.

I wanted to turn away from the screen because I had no desire to experience this again. But my eyes stayed locked on the screen as we moved onto stall six. The camera pointed down at the hay-covered stall, the only one still covered in it. The rustling grew louder as the pile of hay moved in front of us.

"I'm so scared of this last one..."

A creak came from overhead, like something was in the attic above us. We raised the camera up and watched as dust particles scattered from whatever it was. We moved the camera back down and the horrific, monstrous face of a hay

and blood-covered demonic creature stared back at us. Its
hands shot out and grabbed onto the camera. Young me was
out of there at that point. I could hear my footsteps and
screams growing distant.

But current day me was stuck with this demonic thing
staring at me through the TV screen. I gasped and started to
breathe heavy as hell. The thing moved closer, as if it was
going to push through the camcorder and come inside the
living room. It flapped its tongue and grinned—

"*This* is where it all ends, Paul."

I shook myself straight and jumped up from the floor. I
was a scared madman looking for answers. I latched onto the
edge of the flat screen and screamed at the entity staring me
down—

"**WHAT THE FUCK DO YOU WANT FROM
ME?!**"

The demon hissed—

"*Youuuuuuu...*"

Then, the screen turned fuzzy. White noise filled the
Airbnb as I stared back, pale-faced and terrified. Belial was
gone. New footage started... with yesterday's date on it. I
wiped my face, now filled with sweat and panic.

"No, no, no."

There was a twisted home video feel to the new material,
like something out of the movie *Sinister*. But this... *this* was
just *something* sinister. The beginning of a horrific night, all
caught with what felt like an old RCA camcorder. One that
should capture happy memories like Christmas morning or
Birthday parties. Instead, it was three people passed out at a
dinner table: Matt's wife Erin and his two daughters Lily and
Gwen.

The footage cut to an open car trunk. Erin and Lily were
still in there, restrained and in full panic. Suddenly, Matt
returned to the trunk. I quickly paused the footage and stared
at my best friend. His eyes were black, and his lips and skin

were starting to boil away. Like they were exposed to constant heat.

The mystery person was now behind the camera, catching every horrific moment as Matt collected the final two members of his family. We followed him into the barn as he lined Lily up with Erin and Gwen. He tied a noose around Lily's neck and took a step back, revealing the three members of the Roberts family were placed next to open slots in the barn floor.

The mystery cameraman focused on their crying, panicked faces as Matt stuffed their clothes with loose hay. I cried out and begged for him to stop, knowing it was far too late for me to intervene in this scene. Then, one by one, he lit the hay on fire and pushed each one off into the opening. The three ropes tightening and swaying in terror. Moments later, the movement was over.

Just black smoke billowing from the open barn floor.

Matt just stared down at all three with a blank stare. Then, he turned and made his way out of the top of the barn. The camera followed him as he pushed through the overgrown property. A naked, elderly woman ran by in the distance... but Matt and the camera ignored her. They continued to move through the property.

The weeds and rot had grown considerably in the short few weeks since my last visit. None of it seemed to stop Matt or the cameraperson as they pushed through. Branches jabbed through Matt's skin, ripping chunks off as he walked.

My phone dinged again and again but I was too focused on the footage to check it. Matt made his way to the back door, passing the well on his way. The camera quickly focused on the hole, revealing a crazed Alec Munson grinning from bloated ear to bloated ear. Our view returned to Matt, entering the dilapidated back entrance.

He passed the open flooring, revealing crooked, broken steps down into the crawl space. More haunted ghouls

watched as we passed by. Chills went down my spine as I realized this was my first time in over a decade seeing the insides
of the house. We made our way into the living area, now a pile
of wood, debris, and rubble. The ceiling fan was still hanging,
but each fan blade drooped with a wooden sadness.

Like a Jerry Lewis holocaust clown.

Furniture was still strewn about. Kitchen chairs and the
rotted skeleton of a couch stared back, waiting for the attention they craved. Windows were broken and there were holes
in every wall. Weird cult-like symbols adorned the walls. Matt
continued on his way, turning the corner to the unfinished
wooden staircase Hank never completed.

It looked as rickety and untrustworthy as ever. None of
that stopped the possessed Matt, or the mystery cameraman.
They made their way up, slowly revealing the three bedroom
doors waiting at the top of the landing. Only one of the doors
was closed... and it was the one on the left. A big red HELP
was smeared on the front of it.

Luckily, Matt focused on the open doorway in front
of us.

Or... I guess, unluckily.

Still. I had no desire to find out what or who was asking
for help behind that door.

Matt entered the waiting bedroom. The floor was cluttered with old clothes and remnants of my life living in that
space. Another sad ceiling fan. An old, rotted mattress. Empty
window frames. Missing chunks of the ceiling and the walls
literally rotting off. This place was even worse than I had
imagined.

And I was seeing it all through a haunted lens.

Matt stood in the middle of the room, his back to the
camera. A chorus of 8114 whispers and chants filled the
space. It was the scariest, most intense scene I have ever
witnessed in a lifetime of watching horror movies. I wanted it
to stop, I wanted this to be over. I wanted it to—

Matt turned and before I could even react, he slit both

wrists and smiled at the camera. He stumbled forward and peered deep into the camera.

"It's time to come home."

Then, he collapsed to the rotted ground of my old bedroom. And the tape returned to fuzzy white noise. I gagged in horror and let out everything that was hiding behind my eyes and in my stomach. I just witnessed the most horrifying thing I had ever seen in my life. I would never be able to get that out of my head.

The burning bodies of Erin, Lily, and Gwen.

The dying last breath of one of my best friends.

I wanted to collapse and curl into a small, helpless ball. I let everyone down. I caused this. I hurt everyone in my life. I should have never come back. I should have never done this podcast. Or the Adam Benny podcast. I should have never been born.

You should have never left.

Another ding of my phone screamed out.

I wiped my face and hid my cries for the time being. I had ten unread text messages, and they were all from Megan. I stared back in confusion, praying that she was alright. That her family was okay. I swiped the device open, and her messages said the same thing over and over.

PIG.
PIG.
PIG.
PIG.
PIG.
PIG.
PIG.
PIG.
PIG.
PIG.

What the hell did that even mean? Was she calling *me* a pig? Because of what happened between us? More confusion set in, but it was soon interrupted by the fuzz disappearing off the screen and the cameraman turning the camera on themselves. My face went white, and I became dizzy. Absolutely sick to my stomach. I stared back at the possessed, blackened face of Megan. I let out a painful moan and buried my head in deep regret. I pleaded with the screen to admit it was all fake. That this was all my imagination.

It was not.

I watched as Megan disappeared into the lower level of the big barn. I understood what the PIG meant now. I understood everything now. They were *all* waiting for me.

It was time to go home.

Forever.

Chapter Twenty-Two

I parked the damaged rental car in the parking lot of the Mexican restaurant.

I figured this would be less suspicious than parking out in front of the house again. Especially if Chief Allan had anyone out looking for me. I imagine this would be the first stop on the *Find Paul Early* tour. But then again, I still didn't know if what happened with Marion was real. If I had actually pulled away from her headless body or if it was just another trick.

Was any of this a trick?

I wanted so badly for it to be me losing my mind.

For me to be making all this shit up.

I had just spent my morning watching footage of my best friend kill his family and himself. And it was all recorded by my ex-girlfriend. I should call Nick. I should call her.

Maybe I should call Chief Allan and have him send some officers over to her house to find her. To make sure she is alive, and everything is okay. Maybe I should—

I peered into my rearview mirror and spotted a car in the back of the lot. There was a man in it... and he had been here when I pulled in. The way he parked told me he wasn't there for margaritas and chips. He was watching the house.

Was he watching me?

I stared at the side of the house. Everything seemed even thicker in person. I could barely see the side window from where I stood. I was able to walk right up to that window last time and peer into the house. Peeling wallpaper and a magazine covered floor. That was going to be out of question this time. *And that was okay.*

The living room wasn't my destination this time around. I didn't even have to go in the house at all... and every ounce of me wanted to keep that plan. But I knew that was where Matt took his life. I needed to see for myself. There would be yellow tape throughout the property and on the inside. I figured there would also be a patrol or at least officers on watch.

There didn't appear to be any of that as I moved closer to the property. This baffled me.

In the last month, there had been at least five bodies found at 8114. Five people that were all connected to me. Five people that lived here in *this* town. There should be all kinds of law enforcement crawling over this property. And yet, there was no police presence whatsoever.

There was *nothing*.

Just swaying trees and overgrown weeds. A relatively empty parking lot next door. And the occasional chug of a semi engine at the end of the oval-shaped driveway. It was as if nobody thought 8114 was a threat to anyone but me. And those close to me.

Part of me wondered if *this* was the master plan. If *this* was Chief Allan's doing. The Pendleton approach to the classic horror trope where if you kill the main source of evil, everything infected will fall dead as well. Maybe letting this place have Paul Early is the only way all this madness and horror will stop. That's what I've been led to believe by Nancy Hart, Marion Harrison, and Kyle Robinson.

That all this ends with me.

Who's to say that Nancy and Marion didn't share this theory with Chief Allan. Maybe he's out here with the entire department, waiting for me to hang from a rafter so they can all head over to Donnie's place for a cold pint and much needed sigh of relief. And maybe that's for the best.

Maybe I should give everyone a much needed sigh of relief.

The slamming of a car door pulled my focus back to the parking lot. A few distant laughs and a disappearing conversation. I looked back at the car that seemed like it was watching me. I couldn't tell if the man was still behind the wheel or not. Maybe he was there for margaritas and chips after all. I thought back to the night at Donnie's with Megan. To the person who was watching me all night long from the darkened corner. Maybe it was the same person.

Maybe it wasn't.

Maybe it didn't matter.

I pushed through the weed garden and jumped up to the concrete front porch. I stared into the open front door, frozen in fear. I was too scared to go in the last time I was out here. But that wasn't an option this time. **I was going in.**

But I was still allowed to be scared as hell.

The rotting living room floor creaked against my feet. Piles of moldy magazines and old notebooks sat waiting for hands to flip through their pages. Blades had fallen off the ceiling fan. The green and coral flower wallpaper still decorated half of the wall. The other half was either rotting away or covered in black mold. Or missing entire chunks out of it.

I stared into the rest of the house, fear once again taking over. It dawned on me that I was entering the house on the opposite side of the footage of Matt. As if we were now on opposite sides of this journey. Which... we now were. I wondered if mine would end just like his did. Bleeding out somewhere in this place.

Dying in this place I once called home sweet home.

I sighed at the thought. Almost accepting whatever fate awaited me at this point.

I stared out into the big room with the staircase. It looked even worse in person. Bent piles of wood sat against the wall. Trash, clutter, and dirt filled the entire floor. It was stunning to see this place in such bad shape. I caught a glimpse of myself in a large shard of glass.

I was in such bad shape.

I looked awful.

The lack of sleep had caught up with me. But it was more than that. The infection in my arm had spread across the entire left side of my body. The moldy rot was now taking over the side of my face. I looked like fungal Harvey Dent. I felt like my body was shutting down. Like it knew it was back home. Like it was meant to collapse and rot into the splintered wood I used to run across.

Like it was meant to be swallowed whole by this place.

This place.

This is where we lived.

This was a home.

A family made memories here.

And now families are being torn apart by this place.

By me.

I plucked a rotting piece of my cheek off and stared at the black chunk in my hand. It's weird to hold a piece of yourself and not feel anything. This was all so strange. I tried to think of the last time I felt anything. The Kyle news hurt. It felt good to see and connect and... sleep with Megan. It was awful to see what Matt did to himself and his family. But I don't know if I felt anything with any of that.

Like, truly felt *anything.*

I had become numb to all of this. To life. To hurt. To pain. To lying. To causing pain for others. I just didn't care anymore. I was only thinking of myself and well, that person wasn't much to think about these days.

A skittering sound pulled my attention to the old bathroom to my right. It used to lead to my parents' bedroom but now it was just a collapsed opening under the stairs. The sound continued, like a mouse or rat trying to find food. *Or an escape.* I realized it was something much worse.

A pair of eyes watching me from the darkness. They weren't demonic or... human. They were just *there*, watching me from the comfort of the crumpled doorway. They sent a shiver down my spine, and I finally managed to get my legs to take a step. To move me closer to the staircase. They watched me as I slowly made my way up the rickety, unfinished staircase. It swayed under my weight.

Chief Allan mentioned that teens would come in here and mess around. That it was dangerous. I rolled my eyes at the time but now that I'm inside again, I understand it. I understand *all* of it. This wood would collapse under the weight of two people. A small laugh escaped my mouth as I thought back to before this staircase was here.

Hank knocked out the old staircase to build this one. In place of steps, he planted a twelve-foot ladder that led to the upstairs. There was nothing quite like the fear of climbing that ladder with a full backpack on your shoulders. Or shopping bags. Or having friends come over. At least, I thought there was nothing like *that* fear.

I quickly realized I would accept that "fear" again over the one I was feeling at that moment. The one I had as I stood on the upstairs landing, staring at three doorways. Two wide open and the other one closed. I stared at the shut door with the large red HELP smeared on it. My body trembled and I wondered if that was the work of bored teens trying to scare people off. Or if it was something far worse. Something trying to scare anyone off. Trying to warn them to stay away from this entire fucking place. I had no choice—

I had to see what was behind door number three.

I twisted the knob and pushed it open. It looked just like the other two rooms. A filthy, rotted mattress. Old clothes and trash. Peeling paint and broken walls. Old, forgotten memories that were now infected thoughts. This place was polluted now. Forever ruined by the growth of—

Creakkkk...

My throat filled with fear as another creak leaked out of the walk-in closet to my right. I couldn't see inside it from where I was standing, so I had to muster the strength and courage to take another step or two.

I should have never opened that fucking door.

Two bodies hung in the closet, all tucked tight with white sheets. They slightly swayed back and forth but they were clearly... *dead*. I stood, frozen in fear. I had no idea who the faces were behind the sheets. And there was only one way to find out, regardless of how much my mind and body were screaming *don't you fucking dare, Paul.*

I cautiously approached the body in the middle and slowly reached my hand out. I pulled it back, letting my mind get the better of my movement. The bodies stared back, waiting to be revealed. I built up enough courage and gripped onto both sides of the sheet. Then, I ripped it open with every bit of force I could muster out of my moldy arms.

I jumped back in shock. The face of a dead young girl stared back. She looked as if she was somewhere around eleven or twelve. I wasn't *really* sure. I leaned in a bit closer and got a better look at the dead, swaying face in front of me. I suddenly realized who it was—

Sarah Carey.

Megan's daughter. Autumn Robinson's best friend.

I looked at the second swaying sheet. A smaller body. It had to be Grace Carey. I teared up at the thought of Megan's doing this to her own children. The girls she fought so hard for in her divorce with Nick. The ones she would die witho—

Oh Jesus.

I stared at the hanging bodies and felt like the only thing I could do to help this fucked up situation was to pull their bodies down. I carefully unhinged Grace's body from the rope and laid her gently down, clearing a spot on the cluttered floor. I turned and did the same with Sarah. I pulled her down and cradled her over my shoulder, making sure her limp neck didn't fall back—

"Help."

I froze in fear... and turned my head to see the dead face of Sarah staring back. Her mouth ripped open at the sides like wood splintered out of the wall. She tilted her head and suddenly screamed out—

"HELP."

I fell to the ground, dropping her body into the closet. I crawled backwards on my elbows, watching as Sarah's dead, twisted body stared at me. She lunged forward, causing me to fall onto some glass from the broken window. I yelped and looked down, plucking a shard out of my healthy arm. That's when I caught *her* in the reflection of the small piece.

Young Grace was sitting up, watching me through her sheet.

I slowly turned to see black mold spreading inside the sheet. She stretched her sheet-restrained arms out and screamed out at me—

"HELP."

I pulled myself off the ground and ran out of the room, slamming the door behind me.

Holy fuck.

I caught my breath and wiped my eyes. After calming down, I refocused them and looked over at my old bedroom. Yellow caution tape blocked the doorway. I laughed at how ridiculous it was just to tape off one area in this entire hell house. You'd hate for someone to stumble all the way up here and realize something was seriously off with the property.

That something was—

My eyes finally noticed the blood all over the floor. **Matt's blood.** I stared at the stains, trying to process every-thing in my head. Wondering where everything went wrong. How something like this could happen to *him*. I pulled my eyes away and looked out across the ruptured room of chaos. I thought about the old days. This would be the scene in the movie where I see high school Matt playing video games on my couch.

Or sleeping on the floor.

Or laughing his ridiculous laugh, slurping up the remaining bits of a gas station soda.

Not where I see the stains of his body mixing with the discarded rubble of the house.

I felt weak, so I took a seat on the edge of the landing. The HELP door stared down at me, and I ignored the noises of Megan's dead daughters filtering out from behind it. I ignored all the noises in the house. I was only focused on my thoughts and my memory of Matt.

And the loud, boisterous voice calling my name from outside.

Chief Allan stood outside the big open bay window. He stared back at me in full horror. "Jesus, Paul. What happened to you?"

I shrugged and stumbled through the forgotten living room.

"**Everything**," I said, fighting through the pain of moving a mold-infested face.

He looked even worse than he did yesterday, but I'm sure he was thinking far worse about me right about now. When I left the station yesterday, I looked normal. Or, as normal as one could look with lack of sleep and death swirling around. Now, here I was, the wallpaper of my skin peeling away slowly. I held my arm out to the confused man in front of me.

"Last time we were here, you said it was just a small wound. I think it was more than that, Chief."

He looked me up and down, wiping his nervous brow. The trees and weeds swayed around him. I let my arm fall back to my side, flaking a few loose pieces off with the sudden motion.

"You shouldn't be out here, Paul."

I looked over the house as I stumbled closer to the bay

window. Chief Allan was getting nervous, or scared. Most likely both.

"I could say the same for you, Chief."

He nodded, agreeing wholeheartedly with the statement. He eyed the jagged edge of the window and looked beyond me. "You shouldn't be *in* there either."

"Why's that?"

"It's a crime scene, Paul."

I let out a laugh and shook my head. "This entire place is a crime scene. But it's also home."

He rubbed his balding dome and nodded. He knew it was true. He knew everything was true. And yet, here he was. Out here, just like me. But he wasn't just like me. *Not yet anyways.*

"Why don't you come on out here, Paul. I think we should talk about some things."

I sighed and eyed the rotting couch in front of me. I looked over at the walls and the pile of debris. The house was starting to moan quietly, like it wanted me to ignore the Chief. To stay inside. To stay in this place that I had abandoned long ago. I took a few steps closer to the couch, limping on the way. The mold had clearly spread to my legs. I could feel the infected skin flaking off inside my pants. I slowly took a seat and stared back at Chief Allan.

"I'm good, Chief," I said, letting out a deep sigh. "You could always come in here though."

He stared at me through the window, sizing up the situation. I wondered if he had backup on the way or if he had the entire staff camped out in the parking lot next door.

"What did you do to Marion Harrison?"

"I didn't do anything to her. She did that to herself."

"And you just left her... like that?"

Part of me felt relief knowing what happened with Marion was real. I wasn't completely off my rocker like I was starting to think. Still, I left a completely innocent woman's body to fend for itself in front of Nancy Hart's home.

"What was I supposed to do, Chief? Put her back together?"

"Call someone. **Call me.**"

I shifted on the old, rotten couch. The mold was spreading faster now. I could feel it. It was invading my insides and claiming everything in its path. I glanced up and noticed Chief Allan had taken a few steps closer to the backdoor.

"Paul. I'm going to need you to come out here," he said with his best comfort voice. "We can get you some help for... *that*."

That being the infection taking over my entire body. It was surprising that the old Chief still thought this was something natural that could be fixed with medicine. Fixed with the help of a police department which was no doubt about to pin six recent deaths on me.

Shit.

Eight recent deaths.

Nine depending on what happened to Megan when she went back to that damn pig barn. I looked up at the Chief, convinced he didn't know about the two young bodies upstairs.

"There are two bodies upstairs."

He looked at me in shock, unsure of how to move forward with that information.

"Who is it?"

"The Carey girls."

His face dropped in horror, and he shook his head in disbelief.

"Jesus Christ, Paul!"

I shook my head, doing my best to calm his thoughts.

"I didn't do it. I think it was... their mom."

He didn't bat an eye at the comment. He didn't have to. This was the same man who watched footage of Matt Roberts killing his entire family.

"How do you know that?"

"Because she was the one behind the camera, Chief."

He shook his head in disbelief.

"Why would she do that?! Megan Carey is a staple of this community. She's a goddamn saint, Paul. Why would she?!"

"It's like you said, Chief. This place is sick. Always has been. Always will be. It pollutes the mind. Spreads through the entire body." I motioned to myself and the growing virus within it.

He shook his head, fighting the urge to scream as loud as he could.

"Where is she now?"

I waved my flakey, moldy arm up in the air. "Waiting for me out there."

He followed my eyes toward the back barns. I could sense that he didn't know if he should come in here for me or go looking for her. He eyed his radio—

"Chief—"

He looked up at me, now standing from the couch.

"You can't stop what's happening here. What's about to happen here. You can only do your best to contain the spread."

He moved his hands closer to his gun and his radio—

"What's about to happen here, Paul?"

I plucked another piece of skin from my face and tossed it onto the ground, reuniting it with its proper home. The house started to moan louder, like it was healing. The Chief could now hear it as well—

"This place is eating you alive, Chief. Let me put an end to that for you. I'm going to put an end to all of *this*."

He swayed in confusion. "How?"

I nodded my head toward the backdoor and motioned for him to go that way.

"I'll show you. Just help—" I wheezed a hard breath. "Help me get the girls out of here first."

He wrestled with his hands, then shook his head in frustration. "Goddamnit." He pushed through the overgrown brush and branches, then disappeared out of sight. The house continued to moan as I stood inside it. My view of the whole scenario was like a one continuous shot in a movie. The camera was just waiting for the Chief to come around to the backdoor.

Moments later, he poked his head through the old crumbling laundry room. He looked down at the unstable boards leading into the house.

"I don't know about this, Paul. I should go back out front."

I grinned and raised my eyebrows at him.

"Out front? It's far too gone now, Chief. Let me help you."

I limped over to the back door and watched as Chief Allan gripped the door frame. He tiptoed his right foot out onto the soggy wood, feeling the weight out. He eyed me with a look filled to the brim with nerves and fear. I grabbed his outstretched hand, and he pulled the rest of his body in. The house moaned louder, confusing the large man.

"What is it doi—"

I let go of his hand just as he pulled his entire body onto the weak, wooden plank. It snapped under him, dropping his body into the crawlspace below. I stared as the Chief screamed for help. I ignored him and peeled more flecks of skin from my face. I looked over the moldy pieces, filled with specks of facial hair. Then, I flicked it down into the crawlspace just as Chief Allan was pulled under the house in a disgusting, horrific squelch. I looked up from his screaming to see Megan watching everything from the backyard. Then, she turned and disappeared.

The pig barn was calling...

Chapter Twenty-Four

I stared at the two doors leading into the pig barn. Even as my body and mind failed me, I was still terrified of this place. Of these rooms and what was waiting in them for me. I glanced in the left doorway and saw a body staring back at me. It was Megan. Or at least, what was left of Megan.

I slowly entered the space and stared back at her. Eyes and lips blackened with burns; fingernails rotted off. She hissed at me, then smiled. Her voice was deeper now—

"Did you find them?"

I nodded back, letting out a painful sigh.

"How could you..."

"It was for her, Paul. I wanted her to be happy."

Her.

I looked up into the attic of the pig barn to see the outline of The Blackened Lady staring down at us. She was barely visible in the darkened opening, but I knew she was there. I could feel her. *Smell her.* The rot. The burnt flesh. She was watching us.

I looked back at Megan, now standing closer than before.

"You asked how could I..."

I nodded again and she smiled.

"Because she said we could be together forever, Paul."

I looked back up into the attic opening. The Blackened Lady grinned her sinister grin down on us. I shook my head and itched my infected arm.

"You don't want that."

"I do, Paul."

"No, you wanted your girls. Not *this*."

"It's too late. We have each other now. We can have that life you always wanted. No kids. No responsibilities. Just *us*... and this place."

I put my hand on her shoulder and brought her closer.

"I'm not worth it. I'm not worth any of this. You had a beautiful life before I came back into it," I choked up at the thought of everything. "***All of you*** had a beautiful life before I... ruined it. I'm so sorry."

She forced a grin out.

"It doesn't matter anymore. She has the babies now. And we have each other. Isn't that how you always wanted it, Paul?"

I took a deep swallow and tears fell from my eyes as I stared back at the love of my life. This was all my fault. Even before I came back home. Even before all this death. Before Kyle and Matt and Nancy. Before Rachel and Adam Benny. Before this disease overtook me. I was already sick. I was already contagious.

I was already rotten.

I was the virus they couldn't lock up. I infected all these lives with my bullshit. And my constant need for attention. And the things that I wanted. Because that's all that mattered. What I wanted. And none of it matters now.

I don't matter now.

"I don't want that, Megan. I don't want any of *this*," I said, watery eyes and all. She looked up at me with her infected face and smiled.

"None of this is up to you, Paul. Not even *this*."

Before I could even respond, she buried a shard of glass into her neck and pulled it across the skin. Blood exploded out as I fell to the ground in shock. My chest bounced up and down as Megan collapsed to the ground. I looked up to see The Blackened Lady staring down with the biggest smile.

She was happy... and I was pissed as hell.

And heartbroken.

And angry.

"FUCK YOU!!!!"

Fuck all of *this*.

Fuck this pig barn.

And this entire property.

Fuck me.

And fuck the dead face watching me through the wall—

"What the hell do *you* want now?"

Chapter Twenty-Five

I stood in front of the first stall.

My body was withering away as my rotting feet tried their best to keep me propped up. My face was covered in mold, grime, and Megan's blood. I wanted to lay down and catch my breath. Or a break. Whatever came first. But neither one seemed like they were going to be a realistic option. Mostly because the dead Kyle Robinson was staring at me with an annoyed face.

"Hi, Paul."

I let out a small chuckle and gave a slight wave.

"You look awful," I said, knowing damn well that it was a shitty thing to say to a corpse. But he *did* look awful. He seemed to be decomposing at a rapid pace. His skin was nearly all gone. He was just a heap of gray flesh taking up space in the land of the living. If that's where we even were anymore. He smiled a dead smile—

"Have you looked in the mirror?"

I didn't need to. I could feel the way I looked. I could see the sickness on my arms, stomach, and chest. I could rub it off my neck. Pick it off my face. I didn't need a mirror to know my appearance. **I looked like the house.**

Rotted, peeling away, and abandoned.

The insides coming out.

The cover ripping away.

Just the bare bones of what used to be a reliable structure.

I wondered how soon it would be until mother nature claimed me. Burying me with her weeds, shrubs, and trees. Filling my mouth with her dirt. Hiding my bones in this cursed soil. Watching me waste away into nothingness. That last part was already happening. I looked down at my infected arm. A perennial vine was growing out of the original wound and had wrapped around my arm.

"Paul?"

I looked away from my arm and back over at my dead friend. He was now closer, standing only a few stalls away.

"Are you thinking about death?"

A single tear dropped from my eye. I didn't know what I was thinking about at the current moment. Or if it could be summed up in one word. *Death*. There was such a finality to it but there wasn't a finality to this place. To the things that happen out here. If that was the case, I wouldn't be having a conversation with my dead friend. I wouldn't be able to see a dead version of Megan watching me through the gaps in the pig barn wall. I wouldn't be so scared of death.

Scared of *this*.

Of this place.

Of being stuck here forever.

Of The Blackened Lady.

Of Belial.

Of myself.

I was scared and it wasn't of death. That's the only thing I wanted now, **death**. I didn't want to be a rotting piece of 8114 history. Another ghoul for the haunt. I just wanted to lay down and never get back up. I looked over at Kyle, finally answering his question.

"I'm thinking about how much I want that right now."

Kyle crept closer and nodded.

"Soon, Paul. It's almost time," He smiled. "We should talk first."

I nervously eyed the interior of the pig barn. I hated this room. Hated what was waiting for me in stall six. Hated that The Blackened Lady was watching my every move from the attic space. Hated that I had no idea what else, or who else, was watching or waiting for me.

"Here?" I asked, hoping he would suggest a new destination. He grinned—

"For the podcast, Paul."

Confusion overtook my face. Did... my dead best friend just ask if he could come on the podcast? What the fuck is even happening?

"I don't understand," I said, scratching a chunk of moldy flesh from my chin.

"It's about me, isn't it? About this place?"

His face stared back, fishing for the truth. Fishing for my reaction. He took a few more steps closer to me.

"Yes. That was the goal with it."

He nodded, tilting his head in a friendly manner. The kind that said he understood the intention.

"Then, it only makes sense that the final episode happens here. With me."

"Final?"

Kyle now stood directly in front of me. His eyes danced around the barn.

The stalls.

The door.

My face.

My body.

My fear.

He reached out and placed his dead hand on my shoulder. His touch was cold, but it was comforting. It was the touch of a friend. It was the touch of my *only* friend. We both were well aware of that now.

"Yes, Paul."

I shook my head—

"I don't have my gear, Kyle."

"You have your phone."

I painfully pulled the device out of my pocket. Tears started to drop out of my eyes and fall slowly onto the dirty ground of the pig barn. Kyle stared back at the device—

"This is where it all ends," he said, tightening his grip on my rotting shoulder. "This is where the last one happens."

I looked up at his dead eyes. *The last one.* Everything has been leading up to this. It all made sense. The hauntings. The deaths. The demons. That's what the demonic creature in the last stall meant in the video footage.

"This is where it all ends, Paul."

The tears grew heavier. Kyle pulled his corpse hand away from my shoulder and took a deep breath.

"Are you ready, Paul?"

I leaned against stall number six.

Kyle was gone but I was still making good on my promise to him. After we finished recording his interview, he asked me to send the audio file and a picture to ~~Producer~~ Rachel. I was losing feeling in all my limbs, so it took longer than anticipated. Not to mention, the tips of my fingers were starting to rot off. After a few very painful moments, I finally managed to email everything off.

The woosh of the sent file put me at ease. And I hoped that the message would put Rachel at ease. She would know I couldn't hurt her or anyone else again. Maybe it would—

A loud boom interrupted my thoughts.

I suddenly stumbled backwards and fell fully into the sixth stall.

The hay enveloped my body, like I was a kid playing hide and seek with my friends. I plucked a handful of it up and could see that it was now splattered with red. I pulled my crumpled body up to see someone was standing over me. I hoped it was Kyle, so he could tell me what was happening. Or just be here with me as *it* happened. Even if he was a dead, gruesome corpse, he was still a friend... and everyone deserves to have a friend around when they are dying.

And I was in fact... **dying**.

I could feel the blood pouring out of my body and I felt every ounce of the pain that suddenly hit me. I wanted to look down at the fresh wound, just to see if it was only blood coming out of me. Or if it was mold as well. Maybe pieces of the house. I had no idea what was inside my body at this point.

The person standing over me stepped into what little light the barn was letting in. I tilted my head and shrunk my eyes as I leaned up. I wanted to get a better look. Much to my horrific surprise, it wasn't Kyle.

Or Matt.

Or Chief Allan.

It wasn't Megan.

Or my mom.

Or any of the other ghosts of 8114.

It was a ghost of my past, not of my present.

Adam Benny was no longer missing.

He was here, standing right in front of me in the old pig barn. A shotgun hung by his side and tears were dripping down his bearded, tired face. For a split second, irritation washed over me. He shot me... because of a podcast?

What the absolute fuck.

But then, I took another look at the broken man in front of me. He didn't do this because of that stupid podcast. He did this because of me, because of what I did to his life. I ruined it... and it led to his mother dying. And it led to all this pain and hurt.

And it led him here, right to me. The reason for all his pain. **Me.** Paul Early. The reason for so much pain. I let out a pained cough and tried to sit up. The wound wouldn't let me as I fell back into the hay. More of it burying me. I was becoming one with this stall. Blackened, evil, and rotted.

A demonic little thing...

"That was you... at the bar," I asked, growing weaker by

the second. He nodded. "And out there in the lot?" He nodded again, staring back at me with a tilted head.

"It didn't have to be like *this*, Paul."

I gave my own nod—

"I know that."

"But you just wouldn't stop. And then..." Adam did his best to fight back the forming tears, but it was no use. He let them go. He let himself go. Adam Benny became a blubbering mess of a man. I watched him and for a moment, I once again saw the nervous kid sitting across from me at the middle school cafeteria.

Laughing his awkward laugh.

Listening to music.

Trying his best to hide away from the pain of the real world.

I thought back to the last album we listened to together. And the last song we listened to. Radiohead's "Planet Telex." A small part of the lyrics stuck out to me as I sat dying in hay.

You can crush it but it's always near.

Chasing you home.

I crushed Adam Benny and his entire world. And he chased me home because of it.

"I'm sorry, Adam."

He looked down at me, darkened eyes, and even darker thoughts.

"None of it matters anymore, Paul. It's all over now."

I gave him a nod and swallowed my last few bits of life.

This is where it all ends.

"You should leave... before—"

My voice trailed off. I no longer had the energy or strength to finish my words. I wanted to tell him to get out before this place swallowed him up. I wanted to save his life while I could. I wanted to make up for all the wrong I had done. But he stayed, standing over me.

I heard movement and looked above me to see The Blackened Lady and two sheet-covered bodies watching me through the cracks of the ceiling. I saw Megan through the wall, eyes locked on my dying body. Kyle stood in the back door, alone and decomposing. Matt and his family stood in the front doorway, his wife and daughters still smoldering. A deformed, brutalized version of Chief Allan stood behind them. Belial hovered in the corner, watching with red eyes and an evil hunger. My mother watched as well.

They were *all* here for my final moments.

I wouldn't have it any other way.

I looked back at Adam, oblivious to our haunted visitors. I used every last bit of my life to tell him—

"*Leave...*"

He let out a sigh and wiped a string of saliva away from his beard.

"There's no leaving here, Paul. Nobody truly leaves *this* place. You know that."

I did know that. Even when I did leave, this place never let me go. It stayed in the back of my mind. It haunted me. And it took everyone I loved.

And I did the same thing to Adam.

I looked up at him and for a moment, he looked down on me. A million thoughts ran through my head. I wanted to say *so much* to him. But he only said one thing to me—

"Bye for now."

Then, Adam Benny raised the shotgun. He placed it under his chin and pulled the trigger, power washing the old barn ceiling with the insides of his head.

His body collapsed to the ground in a crumpled, dead mess.

Adam Benny is no longer missing.

He was dead... and soon, I will be too.

8114 – Kyle and Paul
June 13th, 2025

Hi everyone.

This... is Rachel McLeod. I know it's been a while since you've heard from me. And I know you're probably confused about why I'm here. On an intro for this podcast. That's... a long story that I'll share another time. Another place. Today is going to be dedicated to a very specific interview. And it's going to be strange for some of you. It's definitely strange for me. And sad for me.

I don't really know where to begin. I stopped working with Paul Early a few episodes into the Adam Benny podcast. It was clear he wasn't entirely honest about that situation or even really cared about the damage he was doing with it. A few episodes after I quit is when everything happened. And Paul went home to deal with the death of his friend Kyle. That's when he launched this podcast. One that he said I was involved with.

I wasn't.

Yet here I am... doing the intro for a new episode of it. **And the final episode of it.** This isn't going to be breaking news for most of you... but I would be doing a disservice to new listeners if I didn't talk about what happened at that house.

By now, it's widely known that Paul Early and Adam Benny were both found dead in one of the back barns. There were four other bodies found at the same time. Megan Carey and her two young daughters... and the chief of police, Chip Allan. A few days before that, Matt Roberts killed himself and his entire family on the same property. A few more deaths in the community were linked to everything that was happening with Paul Early and 8 1 1 4.

It's been horrible for that town. Everyone is looking for answers or a reason.

I don't have that, but I do have something related to what happened. I received an email from Paul Early a few days before his body was found. He sent it on his 43rd birthday... I'm assuming moments before his untimely death. There was a short apology, a picture... and an audio file. The last two send shivers down my spine just thinking about them. The picture of Paul... he didn't look right. He looked sick. Infected. But the file... that's the one that creeped me out the most.

You see... it's an interview that was recorded that day. Between Paul... and his friend Kyle Robinson. The same friend who died on that property days before. It's not long and the audio isn't great but it's chilling. And it will haunt me forever. And I'm going to share it... with all of you.

I don't know what will happen next. Or where this will take me. I'm thinking about going to that town. To find out what happened at that house. To all those people. To Paul. We need answers... and I'm in the business of finding them. The same way this interview found me. It's not an easy listen. And it's creepy as hell. But... it's how Paul Early's story ends.

He'd want you all to hear it. And as you listen, just remember friends, don't forget to clear your head. To give your life and join the dead. To close your eyes and join the black. The things out there?

They'll all come back—

Afterword

8114 was a weird/exciting/scary book to write. And these acknowledgments are proving to be the same. As I write this, I still live in Pendleton, Indiana. It's the town I've called home for more than thirty of the forty or so years I've been on this earth. It's where I went to elementary, middle, and high school. I still pass all three of those buildings on a regular basis. It's a place I spent my summers running around Brown's Pool. Or sitting in the air conditioned public library. Or just riding around town with my friends like a group of midwestern Goonies.

It's a historic town. And it's historic to me.

8114 is part of the actual address that my family and I called home. While the characters in the pages are different, the property is *very* real. The house and most of the barns still stand (*as of this moment*) and it is very much an eye sore on the edge of town. One that is brought up frequently on the town's local Facebook chatter page. And just like the book, it's definitely a headache for the local police force and a source of spooky fascination for curious locals/out of towners. And now it's a source of inspiration.

That house is the *only* reason this book exists.

I started writing 8114 a mere five minutes away from the actual location in July of 2022. I ended up spending the next few months writing chunks of it in hotel rooms in Los Angeles, Virginia, and off the Oregon coast while out on the road promoting the release of *Glorious*. Returning home (in more ways than one), I'd visit 8114 often to take pictures or just admire/mourn what it had become. I finished the first draft of the book nearly a year later in the same spot I started it. At the time, I had no way of knowing that a picture I took of the dilapidated wallpaper my mom hung up in 1991 would be a big part of the marketing of the book. I had no way of knowing that my brother's artwork would appear on chapter headings.

I had no way of knowing a lot of things that would happen because of this book.

Working on it took me so deep... that I found myself writing the 8114 address on paperwork instead of my current address. Spooky/eerie things were happening on the regular. My girlfriend Sophia ended up having an encounter with the same "woman" that my mom had an encounter with in a nightmare she had. My younger brother texted me about a black haired lady who used to haunt him upstairs (regardless of the room he was in). He was completely unaware that I had written the *same* black haired lady into the pages of this book. A few of my other siblings compared reading 8114 to a virtual reality experience... that eerily took them back inside the house in uncomfortable ways. I started having nightmares about moving back into the house... and not being able to get out. 8114 began consuming me and the people in my life.

Just like in the story...

So, *this* is more than just a book. It's a tribute (...*ermmm... an offering?*) to the house and town that shaped me and made me who I am. BOTH have left their mark on me forever...

Now... for the people that are a part of MY story:

Acknowledgments

To my mom and my siblings: 8114 shaped all of us and gave each of us happiness, sadness, scares, scars, memories, and stories to tell. This version of that house and property is the story I wanted to share. It's Paul's story and Paul doesn't have a family. No mom or siblings BUT I'm grateful that I do have ALLl of those things. And grateful that we all have each other.

To Phoenix: It's not lost on me that I'm writing these acknowledgements on the day you graduate high school. After today, you're on a path to new adventures and I can't wait to see where it takes you. Thank you for joining me on impromptu trips out to 8114 throughout this entire process. I love you and I'm incredibly proud of you! Thank you for always being my biggest fan.

To Sophia: Thank you, thank you, THANK YOU. I adore YOU. I'm sorry this book scared you and gave you nightmares. I'm sorry that tree branch out at the real 8114 stabbed you in the arm on your very first visit. So happy you didn't get possessed by a black mold infested haunted house. That would have been so friggin' whack!

To Shannon: Thank you so much for allowing us to put your art in these pages. Your rad demons took this book to another level!

To Eric, Matt, Glenn, James, Jake, and all of the other friends who spent some time at 8114: Thank you for everything. From late night shenanigans... to scary as hell games of Ghosts in the Graveyard (sometimes with actual ghosts. Right, Glenn?)... to MANY failed attempts to spend the night inside those damn barns. Thank you for always coming back.

To Eilise and Nick: Thank you for the constant support and *always* having my back.

To Adam Goldworm: Thank you for being an early cheerleader of this book. And for all of the support and kindness.

To the Early Readers: Thank you for taking the time to read/review 8114. I truly appreciate all of you!

To the WONDERFUL group of folks who took the time to blurb this thing: Michael J. Seidlinger, Clay McLeod Chapman, Laurel Hightower, Phillip Fracassi, Jonathan Janz, Jenny Kiefer. **THANK YOU SO MUCH.**

To Grady Hendrix, John Langan, Daniel Kraus, and Ronald Malfi: THANK YOU for the continued support and kindness.

To ALL of my fellow authors: Thank you for inspiring me. For taking all of us on beautiful and spooky trips to worlds you create. I'm lucky and incredibly grateful to share book-shelves with all of you!

To Booksellers and Librarians: Thank you for giving all of us space on your shelves... and for sharing our stories. You all make the world a better place!

To the Town of Pendleton: Thank you for 30 plus years of inspiration and small town charm. Please don't be mad at me or mad about this book.

To Radiohead: Thank you for *The Bends*... an album that turns 30 years old *this* year. Thank you for all of your other albums. For being my favorite band. For inspiring parts of this book... and for inspiring me.

To my fellow CLASH authors/family who have been so supportive: Michael J. Seidlinger, Brian Allen Carr, Rebecca Rowland, Victoria Dalpe, Eric LaRocca, Cat Scully, and Caroline Macon Fleischer. Go grab all of their books!

To Joel Amat Guell: Thank you for an absolutely terrifying book cover and nailing the horror of 8114 without ever stepping foot in it.

To Kaitlyn Kessinger: Thank you for managing the madness of 8114!

To Brett Petersen: Thank you for the wonderful and detailed edits.

To Leza and Christoph: THANK YOU from the bottom of my heart. I'm so incredibly happy that my debut novel is with you! You both were so supportive and encouraging every step of the way and I'm so happy we get to scare the hell out of readers TOGETHER. Thank you for giving the silly/comedic guy a chance to be serious. Thank you for giving me a home at CLASH. THANK YOU.

To YOU... the reader: Thank you for giving this book a chance... and for giving me a chance. Thank you for constantly giving authors the opportunity to entertain you. To scare you. To wow you. To take you away from the real world for just a little bit. **YOU** deserve all of the thanks.

Also... if you, yes YOU, ever make it to Pendleton, Indiana, my non-specific recommendation is to hit up all the shops/places in town. You can walk everywhere (for the most part). BUT... for my specific recommendations? Here you go:

- Hit up **Falls Perk Coffee House** (125 N. Pendleton Ave) and ask Cat for a 24oz Blended Ice Espresso with Caramel. It's the goods.
- Hit up **The Stable** (105 E. State St) for dinner and drinks. You can't go wrong with their Crab Rangoon Dip, Cheeseburger Pizza, and Old-Fashioned (maybe not together...). Also... they have keg urinals. *The Stable used to be the donnie's Place mentioned in this book.
- Hit up **Good's Candies** (132 E State St) and grab a bundle of S'mores Sticks IF they have them. Good lord.
- Hit up **Jimmies Dairy Bar** (7065 South State Road 67 - *yes, right down the road from* ***8114***) and grab a double cheeseburger platter with a vanilla coke. Throw on a butterscotch milkshake and thank me later. They've been open since the 1950's... and I spent many a summer day melting away on their picnic tables.
- Hit up **Twisters Soda Bar** (3289 W Angle Rd) and get one of their unique beverage creations. I highly recommend the French Lick. *This location used to be where we would have middle school dances. I got punched in the face at one... and stood up at another. Good times!*
- Hit up **Falls Park** for the waterfall and trails... and famous rock that brags about a few white men being hung there. Make sure you make time to swing by the **Pendleton Historical**

Museum while you're there and check out some small town history. It's the same one mentioned in this book! Just... don't ask them about curses or anything like that.

- I HIGHLY recommend visiting during the **June Jamboree** (usually the first full week of June) and waiting in line for a K-Burger. Trust me. You will NOT be disappointed... but you will want another one. So... maybe get two just to be safe.

After all of these recommendations... I know YOU are probably recommending that I hit the gym :)

Finally–

I do NOT recommend visiting the 8114 property but I know some folks will be curious. It's extremely dangerous and unstable. Not to mention... it's creepy as hell. You can get a very good look at it if you hit up the Mexican restaurant on 1251 Huntzinger Blvd. My suggestion? Look at it, nod to yourself that it IS a spooky looking joint... then head inside the restaurant. Order a house margarita and some food... then forget all about the house waiting on the other side of the building.

And do whatever it takes to ignore the whispers and horrors... of **8114**.

About the Author

Joshua Hull is an author, screenwriter, and filmmaker based out of Indiana. He's the co-screenwriter of GLORIOUS, a 2022 Lovecraftian horror film starring Ryan Kwanten (True Blood) and the Academy Award winning J.K. Simmons (Whiplash). He is a past winner of the Edward Johnson-Ott Hoosier Award for his contributions to Indiana film by the Indiana Film Journalists Association. His debut novella MOUTH was published by Tenebrous Press in March 2024. 8114 is his debut novel. Find him on Twitter/Instagram at @joshuathehull

Also by CLASH Books

BLACK BRANE

Michael Cisco

I CAN FIX HER

Rae Wilde

BELOW THE GRAND HOTEL

Cat Scully

SELENE SHADE: RESURRECTIONIST FOR HIRE

Victoria Dalpe

CATHERINE THE GHOST

Kathe Koja

EVERYTHING THE DARKNESS EATS

Eric LaRocca

VIOLENT FACULTIES

Charlene Elsby

THE BODY HARVEST

Michael J. Seidlinger

DEATH ROW RESTAURANT

Daniel Gonzalez

THE LAST NIGHT TO KILL NAZIS

David Agranoff